I0595738

Richard Whiteing

The Island

An Adventure of a Person of Quality

Richard Whiteing

The Island
An Adventure of a Person of Quality

ISBN/EAN: 9783337341299

Printed in Europe, USA, Canada, Australia, Japan

Cover: Foto ©Andreas Hilbeck / pixelio.de

More available books at **www.hansebooks.com**

THE ISLAND

OR

AN ADVENTURE OF A PERSON OF QUALITY

BY

RICHARD WHITEING

LONDON

LONGMANS, GREEN, AND CO.

AND NEW YORK : 15 EAST 16th STREET

1888

All rights reserved

PRINTED BY
SPOTTISWOODE AND CO., NEW-STREET SQUARE
LONDON

CONTENTS.

CONTENTS

THE ISLAND.

CHAPTER I.

OUT OF FOCUS.

Lat. 25° 4′ S.; long. 130° 8′ W.: August 18.

REST, peace, the sounds of a summer noon, and the murmur of waves. The calm of a peak in the Pacific thirteen thousand miles away from the dome of St. Paul's, and completely out of sight of it, if only by reason of the curvature.

I hardly know how I came here. When last I took stock of myself, I was standing on the steps of the Royal Exchange, on another summer afternoon, and looking down. I was busy as usual. I am playing with my little pocket agenda now (perhaps the last I shall ever buy) as I lie here on the broad of my back, and I turn to the entry for that day:

B

'8, Gallop, Row; 9.30, letters, coffee; 10.30, article for " Quarterly "; 12.30, City (I wanted Staples to put something on Turks, and thought I had better be on the spot); 1.30, lunch; 2.30 to bedtime, horse sale, chrysanthemums, calls, club, early dinner, address Working Men's Constitutional Association—" Social Harmonies," dance at Mrs. G.'s, club again, Daudet, bed.'

A mosaic like this is all very well, but a trifle throws it out. When I had done with Staples, I had no further business at the Royal Exchange. I had certainly nothing to do on the steps; yet I lingered there. It was only for ten minutes, but it spoiled my day, and perhaps changed my destiny.

It was such a sight — civilisation in a nutshell — that was what made me pause. I was a part of it, and Apollo was taking a peep at his own legs. Why not? we all seemed to be going on so beautifully; we were all busy, all doing something for progress. What a scene! The Exchange I had just left, with its groups of millionaires gossiping Bagdad and the Irawaddy, Chicago and the Cape; dividend day over at the Bank yonder,

and the well known sight of the Blessed going
to take their quarterly reward ; a sheriff's
coach turning the angle of the Mansion House
(breakfast to an African pro-consul, I believe),
a vanishing splendour of satin and plush and
gold ; dandy clerks making for Birch's, with
the sure and certain hope of a partnership in
their easy grace ; shabby clerks making for
the bun shops ; spry brokers going to take the
odds against Egyptians, and with an appropriate horsiness of air ; a parson (two hundred
and fortieth annual thanksgiving sermon at
St. Hilda's to commemorate Testator's en-
counter with Barbary pirates, and providential
escape) ; itinerant salesmen of studs, pocket
combs, and universal watch keys ; flower girls
at the foot of the statue, a patch of colour ;
beggar at the foot of the steps, another patch,
the red shirt beautifully toned down in wear
—Perfect ! We want more of this in London
—giant policeman moving him on ; irruption
of noisy crowd from the Cornhill corner
(East-End marching West to demonstrate for
the right to a day's toil for a day's crust) ;
thieves, and bludgeon men, and stone men in
attendance on demonstration ; detectives in

attendance on thieves; shutters up at the jewellers' as they pass; probable average of 7s. 6d. to the hundred pockets; with a wall only to divide them from all the turtle of the Mansion House, or all the bullion of the Bank! And, for background, the nondescript thousands in black and brown and russet and every neutral hue, with the sun over all, and between the sun and the thousands the London mist.

It was something as a picture, but so much more as a thought. What a wonder of parts and whole! What a bit of machinery! The beggars, and occasionally the stock jobbers and the nondescripts to go wrong; the policeman to take them up; the parson to show the way of repentance; and the sheriff to hang them, if need be, when all was done. With this, the dandies to adorn the scene—myself not altogether unornamental—the merchants, the clerks, and the dividend takers, all but cog and fly and crank of the same general scheme. What a bit of machinery!

But suddenly the sunlight faded, and there was a change in me. It was not a

change of cause and effect, but only a coinci-
dence. I fancied I saw the man in red fur-
tively writhing in his shirt with the beggar's
itch, scratching himself, so to speak, against
his own clothes. At any rate, something
threw the apparatus out of gear. They
seemed all scratching themselves on the sly.
The whole thing looked as well as ever; but
how did it work? I saw the clerks home,
the shabbies to Stockton lodgings of unstained
brick, where infants down with the measles
called for drink in the night, and querulous
wives compounded that claim for romance
with which every woman born of woman
comes into the world for the not too solid
certainty of bread and butter, at thirty shillings a week all told. I saw the brokers
making for their haven of Bayswater stucco
to receive the reports of Jane's progress in
Elementary Physics, Master Harry's broken
window, the afternoon call of the Bristow
family to bring news that of late Mr. Bristow
has not been feeling quite so well—receiving
these things, I say, and wanting to stamp and
shout, or do something to give a pulse to life.
I saw the sheriff's coach, methought, with

Care in it. There had been another troublesome meeting in Hyde Park; London was going to be governed for Londoners; and tonight's snug Company Dinner, with its guzzling treasurers, masters, wardens, upper wardens, renter-wardens, past masters, chaplains, and the whole batch might be one of the last of the disgusting series. The very policeman had his anxieties; would civic reform bring him down to the wage level of the Metropolitan force? A soldier who had strayed into the prospect seemed to think it was odd to have to guard the Bank on sevenpence a day. They were all scratching themselves; and when an entire civilisation begins to do that, it is a serious thing.

It was a serious thing for me. For the life of me I could not get them into focus again for my grand pictorial composition of a community all playing the game of life for mutual diversion. Theirs was rather that infernal game of bowls in the Fourth Circle, where the tormented wretches will roll the balls in one another's faces, when a more sensible direction would give them delightful sport. I drove home, telegraphed an excuse to the Constitutional Association, and, I am ashamed to say, went to bed.

I was no better next morning. Human society was still out of focus. I describe the complaint with some minuteness, because I believe it is quite a new case for the books, and I may go down to posterity, with my name tacked to this disease, like a second Bright. The anguish is insufferable: it is a sort of intense vertigo, with a very disagreeable accompaniment of sickness in the region of the heart, that robs life of all joy. The men and women about you, instead of having any relation to one another of love, friendship, trust, sympathy, and use, become a mass of gyrating atoms, with nothing but repulsions for their principle of movement. At times you do not know your own brother for such. They form no whole; they will not compose; say, rather, they are out of focus, I come back to that. How to get them in?

I consulted a friend of a most practical order of mind, and, while frankly confessing his ignorance of the complaint, he thought, from my persistent mention of the word focus, that distance might be the remedy. 'You were too near,' he said, 'get further off. Go down to Richmond, and dine.' I thought there might be something in that, and I took his advice. Still it would not come right. So I started for Paris by the night mail.

CHAPTER II.

FURTHER AFIELD.

LONDON was now quite out of the question:
Paris compelled me to be so busy with itself.
I had not seen it for years, and had never
gone below the surface. The tomb of Napoleon, and the view from the Arch (see Guide)
were about the measure of my experience.
This time I found a guide of another kind,
and he gave me a glimpse of the real show.

He put me down at the Flute, a delightful
club, where they try to amuse themselves all
the year round. When they are not fiddling,
at select evening concerts, they are showing
their pictures; and when they are not showing
their pictures, they are holding an assault-at-
arms—the Flute is a great school of fence—
or reviewing the year in a fancy piece, written,
mounted, and played by their own men, in
their own theatre. My Mentor gave me a

month—as he facetiously put it—at another club, the choicest thing there. Through an acquaintance at the Jockey, I found a box-seat on a coach for the private race meeting at La Marche—very pretty, very select; no coming in your thousands, as at the Grand Prix, but just a snug thing between you and me, and a few others, of entirely the right sort. The women looked sweet and fresh as a bed of primroses; the course was like a tennis lawn; we lunched *al fresco*, and no one threw bones on the grass. Far, far away the yell of the bookmaker, and the smell of town. I never enjoyed anything more.

I was presented all round, and was engaged for a reception that night, at the house of one of the chaperones.

'You will see the best salon in Paris,' said A.

'And what is a salon?'

'Well, I don't know; they say nobody knows but themselves. Perhaps a crowd of clever people trying to kill the worm of ennui. Nothing like that at home, where the beast is as sacred as the cow at Benares.'

It was *grand monde* tinctured with literature—that was the social blend. We went to a delightfully old-fashioned house, one of the few left, and saluted a delightfully old-fashioned person—a Marquise, I believe, to complete the harmony of association—who looked like an original of some Moreau le Jeune. Her hair was silver—perfect Louis XV., without the powder puff; she had quick piercing eyes, black amid all this whiteness, and there was a suspicion of hoop in her skirts. She was the queen of a little court, and very condescending. The courtiers acted up to their part by elegant flatteries. They told little stories *at* her to exemplify her wit and spirit, and capped quotations from her last book, in stage asides. The book was just out, and we had learned it by heart that morning, as the inevitable topic of the small hours. It was a dainty *article de Paris*; all her ripe experiences of life distilled in maxim, after the manner of M. de la Rochefoucauld. Every other maxim was about love; they are sometimes too young, but never too old for that vital theme. There was a certain disinterested grandeur in the attitude of the Marquise. 'I too have played the grand game,' she seemed to say, ' and now I umpire the match.'

' " One of the consolations of old age for a woman," said a quoting courtier to his neighbours, " is to dare follow her inclinations without peril of love, and show herself a devoted friend, without encouraging dangerous hopes." Is it possible to speak with more *finesse*? '

' I overheard you,' said the Marquise gaily, ' but you weaken the compliment by talking so loud. I am not old enough to be deaf.'

' For my part,' said the other, ' I want to know how the Marquise found you all out so well, *vous autres*. Listen to this : " Habit has as much power over the nature of men as the unknown over the mind of women." That is my pearl from the chaplet. It is so true.'

' And so finely said ! '

' Ah, all you care about is the workmanship,' said our hostess. ' But I tell you, I have lived all that.'

A General came by, with a charming woman on his arm. He was, in some sort, a counterpart of the elderly muse—silvery hair, a raven brow, and sparkling eyes.

'The butcher of the Commune,' whispered A. to me. 'His column made the fewest prisoners.'

'They are beginning to be troublesome again, General,' I heard the lady say. 'That dreadful meeting yesterday! Did you see the account?'

'We are ready for them, Madame; and with the old argument, mitraille; I assure you they only pretend to like it: it hurts.'

There was a story about everybody—not always a good one; but their worst stories were told in their best way. With us, there is so much ingenuity of subterfuge in the other direction. We might do as well, if we dared. They dare, because the women insist on it, and the sovereign obligation is to keep the women amused—the best women, and best is brightest here. It is a great assault of arms for the gallery, and, if you have a good place, it is pleasanter to be in the gallery than in the ring. The exertion is terrible; some of the most noted performers, I believe, lie abed all next day. You have to justify by gifts, as well as by graces; and the gifts are not always there. Beautiful statues are left on their pedestals : the word tells.

Still, I don't think they make the best of their women. There is, perhaps, a finer use. They try to make the most of them, certainly. The women shape the whole civilisation, and they are just now labouring with much energy at the decline and fall. I have always wondered why they do not include a representation of this commanding interest in the government—*Le Ministère de la Femme.* It would soon rule the whole cabinet, for the incumbent would be sure to know the business of most of the other departments—War, Commerce, Interior, Foreign Affairs.

It is too good for every day—life on the top of a twelfth cake, and some of the figures no more to be visited by sun and rain and the winds of Heaven than if they were cast in sugar. I heard one of them taking the law from another, on the authority of a gazette of fashion, as to the right way of getting up on a winter's morning. There are two ways, it seems. 'An hour before you turn out, *ma chère*, the maid is to light your fire, and put up the screen. Silver lined with pink silk is pretty; it throws a sort of rosy morning light into the room. Mind you have your chocolate on a warmer! And do you know how to warm your toast-rack? A little live charcoal sprinkled with vanilla; it makes the air so sweet. Raoul gave me such a love of a toast-rack (*un amour*) the other day. They are making them in gold now. Don't jump up at once, mind—snooze. What do you wear for a *déshabillé*? I like satin lined with swansdown, and velvet fastenings; buttons are so horribly cold. Line your slippers with swansdown, too; I hate a cold slipper. B-r-r-r! Madame d'Argenson warms her bath-room with little gusts of rose vapour, pumped through a hole in the wall; it is an idea. Do you know how to get warm? Never get cold. Floss silk for your stockings, if you please. I won't even *see* cold. I have my blinds embroidered with a rising sun, and the maid brings in fresh flowers with the chocolate. It makes summer in the room. *Excusez du peu.* Then, if you want to know how happy you are, just lift the blind, and peep out, and see the people dancing on the pavement to keep themselves warm. But you'll see enough of that when you drive, if you like to look at such things. I don't. They are making little things in enamel, for muff warmers, now; tiny apples filled with hot water—not big ones, or you'll spoil the shape of your hands. Besides, big ones would make your fingers red; you only want to make them rosy, *pas trop n'en faut.*

'What kind of gloves do you sleep in? I prefer a plush lining to the kid. Some say swansdown. I think it's *too* warm. Remember there is the coverlet. Stick to plush, you can't do better, from head to foot. I have seen the nightcap fastened with a little cosy turtle-dove, just under the left ear—if you lie on that side. And make her bring you a light *crème de Sabaillon* when you turn in. You know, two fresh eggs, and a small glass of Madeira. B-r-r-r! how I hate the cold.'

A padded person of the sterner sex, who was one of the council, propounded a still more original scheme. '*Chère Comtesse*, why all these precautions, when you might so easily get out of the way? I travel in search of perpetual summer, and find it. My man begins to move south, as soon as the cold threatens here, and the moment he finds settled sunshine, he telegraphs me to come on. I never go till Nature is ready, and, when I reach one place, he starts for another, so I always have sunshine in reserve. We keep steadily flying south till the turn of the weather, and then we make north again for the Paris May. I was only caught twice by rain last year, and once by sleet, and then I threatened to discharge him if it happened again. *Chère Comtesse*, life is too precious: do not waste it in these trials. Will you have a cup of tea?'

'He is very wretched, for all his make-believe,' said Mentor, 'he is going to marry; and he is in a torment of prospective jealousy. It is the funniest case in the world. The young person is faultless; all our young persons are, you know. He pays the proper visits, always in evening-dress—it is our way —and talks to her about the picture-gallery of the Louvre, and the Advent sermons, for just three-quarters of an hour by the clock, with her mother on guard all the time. This is courtship. When she marries, she will acquire the privilege of watching others in the same way, and of being herself unwatched ; and there the retribution comes in. He is not in the least jealous now ; he only knows he is going to be. There are complications, you see. He is not only about to marry the young person, he is very fond of her, which is perhaps inexcusable at his time of life. In the days of his age he remembers his youth, and—*il n'a pas confiance.* He is meditating some domestic ukase about visitors, and positively wants to include his mother-in-law in the family circle. " The duenna, or the cheap defence of households," is, I believe, the idea. All this, of course, implies no suspicion of the lady, but only a most horrible retrospective suspicion of himself. " Do to others as you would not be done by," has been the rule of his joyous life ; and—*il n'a pas confiance.* We used to call him " Proverbs." His choicest conversational effect was a detestable little saying about the folly of acquiring the material of happiness for yourself, when you might always command the stores of your friends. He never quotes his proverb now. I would rewrite the story of Don Juan from his case, with this torment for the Nemesis.

Let Juan marry and settle on this prospect of eternal anguish, and leave old raw-head the Commandant, and his horse, for the nursery tales.'

To a lazy man like myself there is but one drawback in this city; you are rather expected to make love to your neighbour's wife. The nuisance is even greater than in London. They are not exactly rude to you, if you don't, but they mark their sense of your behaviour in a thousand delicate ways. It is considered disrespectful to the lady of the house.

We went to the Opera, and, of course, he led me behind the scenes. It is certainly magnificent. The most self-indulgent monarchs have never enjoyed half so much luxury as these essentially combining people get on the joint-stock principle. They are true democrats, and, as their institutions develop, the poorest will have his *parc aux cerfs*. There is no selfishness in the *foyer de la danse*; all the subscribers are brothers, all equal, all free, as in a temple of faith. *Ces dames* make no distinctions of persons. It was touching to see Army, Navy, Commerce, Senate, and Bar—Bench, I believe, as well—

paying homage at these gauze-curtained shrines. Radical and Conservative leaders, wealthy Jews, the epigrammatic General I had just met, sparks from the club, and some hideous heads of age that ought to have been under nightcaps, were all at their devotions, visiting one shrine after another, sometimes with offerings. *Mesdames* were occasionally wayward and severe, but I am loath to believe that they are cruel divinities, and I am confirmed in this by those who know them best. It was a brilliant scene, the green room itself a blaze of decoration, in ceiling, chandeliers and walls; portraits of great dancers and composers on the panels; grand pictorial compositions above, the War dance, the Country dance, the Love dance, the Bacchic dance; below, a curious patchwork of black coat and white skirt, with here and there a sylph pirouetting for practice, on a floor that slopes like the stage—a fleece cloud driven by the wind—or holding on for support to an iron bar cased with velvet, and pointing, with satin-shod toe, to another and a brighter world. Here, as I have said, Valour reposes after the toils of war, and Legislation after the fatigues of debate. Art sketching in the corner is represented by that solitary, who has a passion for problems, and who is haunted by the desire to transfer this poetry of motion to canvas, and to make the work tremble with life as you gaze. Great soul and genius, the only single-minded one in all this throng—hail!

We looked in at another club on the way home, a mere *tripot* this, but gorgeous like all the rest, and throwing blazing beams across the boulevard from its many chandeliers. Here their industry is *baccarat*, and the net profits of many a mine and factory, transmitted by inheritance to youths of spirit who want to see the world, pass from hand to hand across the baize. Sailors reef the top-sail in storms, coal miners lie on backs or bellies in the dark, girls ripen to premature womanhood in the tropic heat of factories, to feed this sport. I lost a few coins, supped, and came away. One of the players was pointed out to me as the inventor of a new diversion, the Snail Race. The race-course is a smooth board, with a lighted candle at the end, laid on the table in a darkened room. The snails naturally creep towards the light.

There are miniature hurdles, and a water-jump, and the handicapping is done with pellets of clay. You may lose quite enough at this to make it exciting, by maintaining a due disproportion between the amount of the wager and the value of the snail. It is played between five and six, just before dressing for dinner, and it fills in an hour that many find heavy on their hands.

Next day it was a drive in the Bois to salute one's friends. I had already quite a list of them. Surely this people have the secret, I thought, as we span along through alleys of tender green, with sunlight dancing in the leaves, blue and white in the bordering villas, and the purple slopes of Valérien to close in the scene. We skipped the Lake, according to directions, and looked out for faces under the acacia trees. They were all there. I was so delighted with it that I could not go indoors; so we pushed on, by the Cours la Reine, and the river, to see more.

They have the philosophic taste for angling; the banks were lined, yet the waters lost nothing by their sport. It was live and let live, with man and fish. We had left the black coats behind us; they were blouses now; and everywhere the white and blue and green, the brightness, and the leisured groups. A worthy pair of retired *rentiers*, male and female, seemed to have devoted the whole afternoon to washing their poodle in the Seine. Monsieur lathered him, and drove him into the water for the rinsing with innocent oaths and ejaculations, '*cré nom! bigre! saperlipopette!*' or whistled him back with a properly certificated dog-call, when he seemed to be going out of his depth. Madame stood by with towel, comb, and brush. For this they had kept the little grocer's shop at the corner of the Rue St. Jacques de la Boucherie for seven-and-twenty years, and toiled late and early, Sabbath and fête, and put savings in the Paris Loans! 'And why not?' I ask, with ever increasing emphasis, while anyone shall say, 'And why?' All classes seem so happy, I thought, so innocently gay—it is the stock reflection of the tourist in the Paris streets.

I was standing on the bridge; and just then there was a rush past me of the *avant-garde* of a crowd, followed by the main body. They were fierce-looking and sorrowful. Those who were not in blouses wore grease-polished coats and hats—always a bad sign —and the few who were not frowning had the grease in their smile, always a worse. There was a woman at the head of them, in black, and carrying a black flag, an angular creature, as lantern-jawed as a saint from a missal, with eyes like live coals.

' What is it ?   Who is it ? '

' The Red Virgin.   We want bread, *citoyen.*'

It was not literally true, I think—most of them looked fat enough—prospectively true, perhaps.   They hurried off towards the outer boulevards, I following, and, on their way, they pillaged a baker's shop, the Black or Red one standing by, and waving her corpse-flag with approval, but touching no morsel of the food.   Then they poured into a dirty little hall, garnished in the vestibule with a col-lection of pamphlets inciting to murder and arson, and began to ' meet.'

They had a clear issue before them, and they knew their own minds.   They were met to see how they could burn down civilisation.

Nothing more, nothing less. Government was to go, property, laws, classes, the whole framework, with all the pretty things I had lately seen—the drag that took me to La Marche, the salons, the Opera, the coaches in the Wood, myself too, I suppose, by implication, though none took notice of me. They spoke with beautiful volubility, precision, logic, each man perfect in the spouter's gift.

Presently the Virgin in black rose, and I began to understand why she was called the Red. She spoke in sing-song the chaunted dirge of the thing they wanted to burn. It was very grotesque, and very serious. 'Citizens, it must all go, only the fire can purge it. Nothing will better it ; it has been bettering for eighteen centuries, and it is worse to-day. I believed once, like them, and wrote hymns to the other Virgin, and I know she never hears. She is made of stone, like their hearts. O citizens, the infamy of it !— their fine houses and fine feasts, fine adulteries and fine lies, with labour for their everlasting bond-slave and thrall. *Voyons !* it is all a mockery. How many of you, before we broke the bread shop open, had eaten to-day ?'

' *Moi!* ' shouted perhaps twenty voices, and about as many hands were held up, while about five times as many were held down. ' If there were only one,' said the Red Virgin, ' we would burn it for that one. What! with ships in every port, and the finest climate and soil in the universe, and all the labour and all the martyrdom of the past behind us to start us fair, we cannot give every man his crust and his cup of wine! *Voyons : on se moque de nous!* Stand out of the way, with your governments and your religions, and leave us to ourselves, to be good. We should be so good without you. It would be so easy ; love comes naturally to man, and justice; only the *laws* of loving and the *laws* of justice bar the way. The codes are between us and the Sun. Burn them, and start afresh. *Vive l'Anarchie!* '

' *Vive l'Anarchie!* ' cried most of us, but it was not *nem. con.* ' Down with the Virgin,' shouted a big, black-muzzled fellow near the door ; and he meant the Red one too !

' *A la porte l'espion!* ' roared fifty others back at him. It was a fight.

He was not alone—' *à bas la Vierge!* ' re-

peated his body-guard, closing round him.
The chairs were broken into fragments in an
instant, and I was luckily able to interpose
my walking-stick between one of the fragments and the head of a prostrate man.

So they fell to buffets, the troubled souls
who had met to settle the new law of love,
beating each other cruelly with hand and
foot. It was clear possession, and their tor-
mentors were, perhaps, the self-same legion
that once did duty in the swine. They tore
each other, in sheer impatience for the rise of
the curtain on the great poetic drama of the
Millennial Reign. They had bad seats for the
show, I think; that had something to do with
it; in the comparative airiness of the boxes,
patience does not come so hard.

I strolled away. Out of focus, too, this
group of humanity; and worse than the
last!

CHAPTER III.

FLIGHT.

I WAS really running away now. It was not retreat, but flight; useless to pretend that I was even looking civilisation in the face.

Some instinct led me to Geneva. There would be safety, I thought, in its balanced poetry and prose, the mountains held in check by the tourists, the lake by the hotels.

But I had reckoned without the gentleman whose crown I had saved in the late *mêlée*. He turned up one day on Rousseau's Island, and hailed me as a brother. I assured him I was but a second cousin, at the outside. It was in vain. He led me to a remote garret in the old town, and introduced me to a circle of blood relations in democracy, by whom, after examination, I was received into the family.

I did not mind; only it was hard to find this sort of thing going on everywhere.

I was evidently found to improve on acquaintance, for, one day, I was solemnly invited to a polyglot tea party, in another garret, with a Russian lady making the tea.

It was green tea, fortunately; else it would have been altogether too absurdly innocent a compound for this entertainment. Everybody but myself had done something, and I felt quite ashamed to say that I had only stood on the steps of the Royal Exchange. My sponsor came out in a new light; he had been first smearer of petroleum at the Ministry of Finance, during the Commune. He assured us that no other building burnt half so well. He laid it all on the *rez-de-chaussée*; his colleagues wasted their stuff on the upper walls. A friend from Spain had shot three priests in the Carthagena riots, with one discharge of a blunderbuss. There was an offer to introduce me as one of the gentlemen who tried to sky London Bridge, so that I might not look strange, but I hate a false pretence. The lady at the samovar was a student emissary, who crossed the frontier with despatches, and she had just come back with news. She had seen the latest execution at St. Petersburg—

two of the brethren and one sister hanging
up in the falling snow, as stiff as frozen ox-
tongues. There were other cheerful reports
from Rome, and from Belgrade ; and one com-
panion, who was strong in geography, gave
us a bird's-eye of the whole woeful earth. It
was to much the same effect, only that, further
afield, the dull pain of living was oftener met
by endurance than by revolt. We had five
minutes in the native quarter at Amoy, and
saw an ingenious device of the needy to qualify
as mendicant cripples, by making their feet
rot off. It is something of a trade secret ; but
the right way is to tie a cord tightly round
the ankle, till the member mortifies. It is
a living—where it is not certain death. Next.
we were with the stark naked casuals, squatting in the streets of Pekin in winter time,
while, gorged with humanitarian learning, the
lordly scholars pass. We came home by way
of Central Asia, and dropped in on the squalid
poor of Smarkand lousing among their quilted
rags. The coaling coolies at Aden detained
us but a moment ; and, but a moment more,
the sponge divers of the Ægean, with their
lungs choked with blood, for the great law .

of the margin of subsistence reaches even to the ocean bed.

Next day, I made straight for Genoa. I seemed to labour for breath on the dry land, and to want the sweet clean sea.

There was an Italian merchantman in port, fitting out for a voyage round the world. They had macaroni on board ; and, if they had boiled the huge cargo, they might have girdled the globe as they sailed. They were going to take it to Ceylon and the Philippines, by way of the Suez Canal, and then, come back by the Horn to pick up something for the home market. I wanted a ship ; they were not averse to a passenger. Short of ballooning, it seemed the readiest way of giving Civilisation the slip.

We sailed ; and, as I just had the honour to inform you, here I am, on a peak in the Pacific, and thirteen thousand miles away from the dome of St. Paul's—which, as everybody knows, is but a stone's throw from the Royal Exchange. For distance, I think this will do.

CHAPTER IV.

ADVENTURE.

How I got there, this chapter will tell.

The calm of that passage of the Indian Ocean!—the days of sunlight, a little too ardent, perhaps ; the nights of moons—the calm of the spirit, I mean, profounder than the calm of waters. A ship is either a heaven or a hell; and when it is a heaven, why not let that one suffice? The world empty. and no papers—no daily report from the sick bed of civilisation. Who could want more, or less ?

Ceylon, with its new faces and its shipman's bustle, hardly ruffled our repose, and when it did, I shut my eyes. At the Philippines, it was much the same. Both are fully described in the Gazetteers.

Then it was hey ! for the next long lap to the Horn, with only a call for water or for wild-fowl, here and there. We were in the Pacific now, for all its bursts of temper how finely named! Should not all oceans, boreal or equinoctial, have the same generic title, for, spite of storm and reef and waterspout, surely their message is peace? Such stretches of proud, self-sufficing silence in between the gusts, such comforting assurance, in deepest whispers, of the final rest! Here, on salt water only, can we set compass for the land voyage. Now and again it thundered, and the rain crashed down like falling walls of water, but always my soul was still. If the worst happened, we should still reach the deepest bottom at last, and find a soft bed in the ooze.

There was magnetic disturbance of a kind, however, in that Italian skipper. He was not too well acquainted with the course, and he was subject to scares about cannibals. He feared that the natives of these parts might prefer him to his macaroni. He had an old Genoese edition of Cook, and he read it as if it were a deliverance of yesterday. Whenever we touched at an island, existence seemed hardly worth having at his price of precaution —scouts, and rear-guard, and main body, all to effect a positive life insurance against some old woman squatting on a mat. Poisoned arrows, again, were his peculiar aversion, and, to keep out of reach of them, he usually directed landing operations through a trumpet from the ship's side. In vain I argued that one fear ought to preclude the other, and that, if they poisoned him, he would certainly never be fit to eat. Sometimes I tried to reassure him by landing alone, and returning with an escort of friendly natives, and a store of yams. The lesson was lost on him; he attributed my safety to the fact that my joints offered no temptation to the critical eye.

One glorious afternoon, sailing from the south we saw a peak rising sheer from the ocean and huge, for it still might be about thirty miles off. It seemed to taper from a broad and solid base, like the summit of a cathedral. He said, ' St. Peter's.' I said, ' St. Paul's.' As we got nearer, we made out a small island of solid rock, with sharp precipitous sides, plumped down in the blue, and with no neighbours in sight. Add Kensington Gardens to Hyde Park, and you might have its total area. It was covered with verdure and stately trees ; but a fringe of white at the water's edge showed that, in spite of the perfectly calm weather, the surf was boiling against its awful shores.

It looked fruity, though desolate, and I insisted on going ashore for guavas, much to the disgust of the skipper. He offered me dried plums, in dissuasion, from a box fringed with paper lace, but the sight of them only increased my craving for the fresh fruit. At last he let me put off alone, crossing himself as I left the ship's side ; but he had done this so often that it made no particular impression on me. I promised to be back in three hours at the outside, while he stood off and on. There was no anchorage for us, even if there had been time to let go.

The little place grew in beauty as I neared it, but in grimness, too. Below the verdure, it was all great fangs of rock, biting into the sea at the sharpest angles. The surf was more terrible than ever on a closer view. The water was flaked with the fury of its strife with the iron-bound shore. I thought of turning back, but I am very fond of guavas.

Besides, I had seen something of the management of boats in surf, and I fancied it was
easier than it looked. The knack is to mount
the crest of a wave, and shoot in with it into a
soft place. There was one soft place here, in
the angle of a little bay, with earth and wild
plants sloping to the water's edge, and for
this I made. I thought I was doing it very
nicely, until I felt a heavy blow on the head,
and, just before my eyes closed in a dead faint,
saw the boat, bottom upwards, floating out to
sea. I had missed by a hair's-breadth, and
brushed a boulder half hidden in the grass.

The moon was up when I came to. I
must have lain there some hours, wedged
comfortably in the brushwood that clung
to the stone, high, and nearly dry again,
though at the outset I was, of course, wet
through. It was a mercy rather than a judgment, after all. The sea had shot me out of
its own reach, and no one could have been
more considerately stunned. There was a
slight flesh wound on my forehead, but no
bone broken anywhere. I sat up, and brought
my thoughts back to life ; then slowly found
my feet, and went to look for my hat. In a

few moments I became aware that there were
other things missing, namely, the boat and the
ship.

All were gone. The great stretch of sea
was without a speck. I was alone, abandoned
to starvation or other miserable death. I
threw myself on the ground and sobbed.

What had become of the ship? Alas! my
theory of probabilities was only too easy to
form. They had found the upturned boat,
and perhaps the hat, had jumped to the
conclusion that it was all over with me, and
made off, pursued no doubt, in fancy, by a
fleet of cannibal canoes. And here was I, a
second Robinson, on a lonely shore, without so
much as a wreck to start me in housekeeping.

The rock sloped at this place, as I have
said, and I easily climbed to the summit, and
looked around. I meant to sit down there,
and form plans. But I forgot all about the
morrow, as soon as I saw what nature had sent
me that night. It was the full moon; and to
know what moonlight is you must come to
these Southern seas. I had no print to read,
but I could trace the lines in my palm, and I
was consoled by the observation that my line

of life was a long one. Behind me were the massive shadows of higher hills, before, a table-land of grass and wild trees, bathed in the soothing light, and beyond, the molten silver of the sea fringed with the everlasting surf. The only landward sound was the soft ' click, click ' of some native bird. It was impossible to feel sad ; it was a place to die in, if not to live in, come what might.

The night was warm, I felt no chill, and I sat down and thought the thoughts one thinks in the moonlight. The pity of it that one should ever take the trouble to be less than one's best in this passing flash of life! What matters the pain for the purchase of this certain joy—the only joy that is sure, so why not make the most of it in valour, honour, fortitude, without waiting for aught sweeter in the dim beatitudes beyond ? So to live as, at this moment, thou couldst cease to live ! It is the moon's message, delivered with unfailing regularity once a month, and her main business is to deliver it, not to suck up tides. The shilling almanacs will never contain everything till they devote a line to this interesting fact. When the moon gets that message into the soul,

all else must make way for it. Stockbroking
seems a pity, in her mildly searching light, with
most other modes of getting on ; and no wonder
there is a tradition in Bayswater families that
this kind of natural illumination is bad for the
eyes.

I, too, was not unmindful of a domestic
tradition on the subject ; and, when I felt
sleepy, I sought the shade of a hill. I made
my bed of brushwood, and sank down. I
ought to have felt cold, and caught cold, but
I did neither—perhaps the very dews were
pickled by the sea air.

The sun called me betimes next morning,
and I rose at once, painfully hungry, but in
perfect serenity of mind. Now that I saw
more of my new home, I could not think of it
as my grave. Before me, to the north east,
rose the tremendous peak we had sighted
from the sea. The hills into which it sank at
its base stretched right across the island,
forming a ridge at right angles to the other
previously seen from the ship. I was thus
shut in a corner, and I could see nothing of
what lay beyond. I might have seen more
by mounting the hill, but I seemed to dread

to do it. I thought I would follow the coast line, from a vague idea that it would be safer to have the sea at hand. There was no sign of human life, but the air was alive with myriads of sea birds, wheeling about the rock. The fly catchers, darting through the air for breakfast, added to the animation of the scene, but, of course, made me feel hungrier than ever. There was a distant prospect of a meal, however, in the wild goats looking down on me from the hills—in grave wonder, I hoped, at their first sight of a man. Early as it was, tiny lizards darted about at my feet in evident distress of mind.

Always skirting the rock, I came soon to another peak, lower than the one first seen, but still awful in its sheer fall of six or seven hundred feet right into the sea. I lay down, to peep over the almost perpendicular wall, and rose again with a sense that I and my island were going to be very cosy together, and all to ourselves. Then, lifting my eyes to the highest summit beyond me, to measure the breadth of our domain, I saw a human shape, standing clean and clear and quiet on the verge, against the cloudless sky.

CHAPTER V.

RESCUE.

It was a woman—so much I could make out, in spite of the distance, some three hundred yards as the crow flies, though more, of course, by the dip between the two hills—a woman, by the rounded contours of the silhouette, and a tall one. Of her face, I could as yet say nothing : she was looking out to sea.

A woman, then, but of what tribe? There was no telling by the dress. She wore a petticoat of some dark material, reaching to the knee. It was but a dark patch, of course, as I saw it ; and above it was the white one of another garment. At first, that was all I made out—the patch of dark, the patch of white, with the half tint that stood for her bare limbs. She seemed to be shading her eyes with her hand, as she stood in the glare of light.

Suddenly she wheeled round, as though to descend the peak, and, in doing it, saw me. We were now face to face, she on the higher summit, I on the lower, with only the valley between us. I could not see her features, but she seemed rooted to the spot with astonishment.

I instinctively felt for a weapon. I expected a scream or a signal, and savage warriors trooping over the hill. But she made no sign. Hesitation was out of the question: I moved straight towards her. I had no beads about me for a peace-offering, so I fumbled at my watch chain, and wrenched off a propitiatory pencil-case that I hoped might serve.

She advanced too. Then, at every step, the bands of light and dark began to develop into the most majestic shape of youthful womanhood I had ever seen. The white was evidently a sleeveless undergarment reaching, like the petticoat of deep blue, no further than the knee. The naked arms, legs, and feet were no darker than the cheek of a brunette.

The chemise was low, and above it rose the glorious bust, almost as broad as a man's, and with a virgin firmness of line that was strength and softness too. She was very tall for her sex, tall even for mine, but the perfect proportion between body and limbs took off all effect of ungainliness. She moved with the beautiful poise and precision of a mountaineer, brushing hillock, tuft, and boulder in the slope, as though they formed but one level.

Would she attack? It looked so, else why had she met my advance so boldly, without calling her tribe? She seemed to have taken the measure of me for single combat. She would have been a formidable foe, in any case, to say nothing of the handicapping in respect for the sex.

But there was no more of aggression than there was of flight in her attitude, as she paused at last, when but a few feet parted us, and looking down on me in placid wonder, from large and lustrous eyes, showed me the peculiar beauty of her face. Her features were regular, without being faultlessly, or rather, faultily so. Her complexion would have passed muster for fairness in Provence, if not farther north. The only signs of race type were in a certain prominence of the brow, and in the deep liquid softness of the gaze. I had seen such eyes in some of the Coral Islands, and I used sometimes to wish we could take a pair of them back with us, to put the Italian women out of conceit with their own. Her lips were rather full and sensuous, but this did not impair the tender dignity of her expression. Her dark hair, shining, I regret to say, with some native oil, which, even at a distance, I could perceive was scented, seemed to have been caught up with one sweeping gesture, and gathered in a knot behind. Her feet were rather large, though perfectly formed ; and she had drawn them close together, as she paused, like a child toeing the line in school. To complete the similitude, she stood perfectly straight, with her arms folded behind her, and her head thrown back—her bosom, the while, gently rising and falling with excitement but half suppressed, and carrying with it, in its motion, her sole ornament, a common English navy button, fastened with ribbon to her throat. I had looked on other women as beautiful in feature, but never on one so magnificently formed. It recalled poetic ideals of the youth of the race.

Evidently she was waiting for me to say something, but how was I to say it? The whole Melanesian mission might have been at fault in the speech of this solitary isle. So I began toying with the pencil-case once more, and then, in a desperate attempt to recall some characters of a universal sign language, I folded my hands on my breast—as I had once seen it done by savages of wilder aspect, in a ballet in Leicester Square.

No language in the world could do justice to my astonishment at what followed, and therefore I set it down without comment, just as it passed.

'You speak English, I suppose,' said the girl. 'How did you come on the Island?'

The accent was as pure as yours or mine; in fact, there was no accent; and the voice was as soft as the eyes.

For some moments I could utter no word. I went on with the sign language, but then, only to pass my hand over my brow.

'Who are you? and how did you come here? We saw no ship from the Point!'

'Madam, I——'

The gravity of the features relaxed, and the girl laughed.

'I knew you spoke English; but why won't you go on? Oh, how stupid I am! You are faint and ill. Lean on me, and come and have something to eat.' In another moment she was by my side, with one strong arm round me, and nearly lifting me off the ground, in the attempt to help me to walk—a most humiliating reversal of protective rôles.

'I can walk perfectly well, thank you; please let me go,' I had to say, like some coy schoolgirl in the grasp of a dragoon. It was very ridiculous, but I really could not get free.

'Very well, then, but I will carry you when you like. Now, tell me who you are, and please don't call me Madam again. Victoria is my name—after the Queen— "Victoria."'

—'By the grace of God,' I could not help thinking, remembering what I had feared, and what I had found.

'Victoria, I was nearly dashed to pieces on these rocks last night.'

'Where is your ship?'

'It was over there, but it has sailed away.'

'On the south side. But don't you know that the landing-place is on the north?'

'I know nothing. I never thought to find a living, still less a civilised, soul in this place. Tell me where I am.'

'You don't seem to know much geography,' she said, with an offended air. But she was mollified in a moment. 'How faint you must be! Lean on me. If you don't, I will carry you, whether you like it or no. Poor thing!'

I wanted no support, but I was nothing loath to lean upon Victoria. So we walked away, with an arm round each other's waist, as innocently affectionate as the primal pair.

She led me towards another slope of the Peak, and, all too soon for me, with such leading, we reached the top.

The whole island lay before me, from sea to sea, quivering with life in the morning sun. In its irregular outline, it seemed like some quaint sea monster that had shot up from the depths of the Pacific to take a look round, and that might instantly disappear. It was head and shoulders out of the water, joining the sea almost everywhere at the base of perpendicular rocks rising to heights of from four to six hundred feet, and it had little or no beach. On all sides, the wave seemed in fretful strife with the rock, but beyond the broken lines of surf lay the calm of the immeasurable ocean, with nothing in the way, it seemed, between this and the next world. The range of hills cutting the island in half from east to west sloped to the edge of the cliff; on the southern side, in deep valleys, filled with plantation plots; on the northern, into two terraced spaces, one above the other, commanding a view of the sea. On the highest of these lay a settlement of civilised men, its cottages lapped warm, like birds in their mosses, in exquisite vegetation—palms, and banyans, and cocoa-nut trees, and, as I might guess, by what was nearer to the view, passion-flowers, and trumpet vines, and creeping plants of infinite variety, the rich growth clothing even the adjacent summits and hillsides, and the sharp inaccessible slopes, right

down to the water's edge. Below the settlement, on the lower terrace, was a grove of
cocoa-trees, with no habitation, and below this
again, a little bay, evidently the landing-
place, and the only one on this cruel shore.
All this beauty of nature and homely sweet-
ness of ordered life, lying to the north of the
dividing ridge, had been hidden from me in
my rude landing-place, even the cultivated
valleys being shut out by a transverse section
of the rock.

We were still standing on the hill when,
from a clump of cocoa at its foot, a little girl
came running towards us—a reduced copy, to
scale, of Victoria, in build and strength and
perfect animal grace. Without standing in
the least upon ceremony, she gave me a most
hearty kiss, and asked me my name.

'I wonder now if you could read it,' I said,
feeling in my pocket for the card-case which
I had kept by me in all my wanderings, and
extracting from it a card that showed woeful
traces of the ducking of the night before.
The little one's eyes dilated in wonder as she
read the inscription, and in one swift glance
took me in from head to foot. Then she

turned, and started for the village, at break-neck speed down the steep incline, shouting as she went, 'Mother! mother! Here's a lord!'

In a few moments she was mounting the hill on the other side, to the first terrace, and I lost her for a moment in the cocoa grove. She emerged into the second steep path that led to the settlement, still uttering her strange cry. I could see the doors' opening, the people turning out, the terrified flutter of domestic fowl.

'Come!' said Victoria, and she strode on in the track of the child, turning now and then to help me. We soon reached the level of the grove, a majestic scene, roofed with branches, and carpeted with shrubs spangled with the sunshine that shot through the trees.

I sank down in the delicious shade, not caring to go farther, not caring to speak. I was more faint than ever, for, in spite of the excitement of the adventure, my long fast began to tell.

An opening in the trees showed the path to the settlement, with fifteen or twenty villagers trooping down under the leadership of the infant herald, who waved them on with my card. There were women and children, and, this time, men, most of the latter fit mates for Victoria in frame and stature. Their shirts were armless, their trousers reached only to the knee, all beyond was bare bronzed skin. They looked all strength, suppleness, and abounding health.

A dozen began to talk at once. ‘How did you get him, Victoria?’—‘All last night!’—‘Oh, the poor thing!’—‘How white his skin is!’—‘Is he a real lord?’—‘Let me give him a kiss!’—‘Has he had his breakfast?’—‘He must stay with us.’—‘No, you had the last one.’—‘With me!’—‘Me! Me!’—It was like a clamour of children, but it was stilled in a moment on the arrival of an elder, dressed rather differently from the others, and for whom they all made way.

‘Father,’ said Victoria, addressing the old man, ‘I won’t give him up to anybody. I found him, and he belongs to me.’

‘Take him to my house,’ said the Ancient, ‘and none of you speak a word to him till he has had something to eat. Here, Reuben, lend a hand;’ and he nodded to a young fellow standing at least six foot two. who lifted me to my feet as one might lift a child.

It was time, for their talk began to come to me like a far-off buzzing. I walked as in a dream, but I was aware of a hushed crowd, a beautiful path through the trees, a green lawn on the summit, bordered on three sides with houses of dark wood and thatch. embowered in gardens that scented all the air. Into one of these houses I was taken, and laid on a comfortable couch.

'Where am I?'

'Hush!' said Victoria. 'You are in the house of the chief magistrate of Pitcairn.'

CHAPTER VI.

BEARINGS.

Pitcairn! I remembered something of what
the word meant, next morning, when I woke
from a refreshing sleep.

Who does not know that story, just a century old? A ship of war from England sent
out to these southern seas to fetch breadfruit
for transplantation. Her work easy, her crew
passing long delicious enervating months in this
contrasting clime; the southern sky, in lieu of
our murky heavens, the southern woman, in
lieu of Deptford Poll. Then, the breadfruit all
collected, the signal given to start for home,
but given by an unpopular commander.
Mutiny next. The captain and a faithful
remnant thrust into an open boat, with a hand-
ful of provisions; the crew gently sailing
away in search of some happy isle. One
group thinking they had found it in Otaheite,

and there disembarking, leaving the others to
steer further forward into the unknown. These
last, finally, spying the dot of Pitcairn, and
stopping there, scuttling their ship to signify
' Good-bye ' to the world. An auspicious
settlement, with all the comforts—the heathen
woman (imported) and heathen whisky, home
made, by an inventor of genius, who could
not find even this morning light sufficiently
exhilarating without his dram ; a few native
men for service, beside. So, they began to
be happy for ever, according to the most
approved methods of Wapping Old Stairs.
Meanwhile, the captain and his faithful remnant, in the open boat, make the best of their
way to England, through sun and storm ;
their first halting stage, and nearest prospect
of relief and refreshment, twelve hundred
leagues away, their rations weighed to the
twenty-fifth fraction of a pound, and a cocked
pistol always ready for service between the
rotting bread and the famished crew. Home
at last ; the story told ; and another war ship
sent out to the Pacific, to pick up the mutineers. The Otaheitan settlers, or what is left
of them, caught and brought back to hang,

or otherwise pay their score ; the Pitcairners never found by the avenger, though she rakes the seas for them for months. Nothing heard of them for close on twenty years, when, one day, in the following century, a Yankee skipper, ranging the smooth ocean, finds this speck of volcanic eruption on its face ; and then the whole story comes out. We left them, it may be remembered, with liquor and ladies, sunshine and a solitary isle, the honestest attempt ever made to realise the nautical ideal—said sometimes to extend to other professions—of a paradise ashore. Alas ! it still was not enough. There had been wild debauchery in both kinds ; riot and midnight murder; sudden and crafty slayings, to the confusion of all method in the butcher's art, of men by women, women by men, Englishmen by natives, and contrariwise, then, of Englishmen, among themselves. At last, only one man is left, and he of our stock, with twelve native women in his guardianship, and nineteen children, most of them fathered by the Englishmen dead and gone. This man, struck with horror and remorse, takes a turn to piety, and, knowing nothing of heredity, is simple enough to believe that God gives the race a fresh start with every generation. So believing, he reclaims this spawn of hell to Christianity and civilisation, and makes a new human type. Other varieties may yet be found in the stars; this one owned a virtue that almost ignored evil, and that was well nigh as effortless as the love of light. It was strong and gentle, truthful and brave, by fine instinct; it had an untaught facility of laughter and of tears; was passionate in loving, yet strange to violent hate—an image of character that cast no shadows, the most wonderful curiosity in life.

The Yankee skipper soon made his strange discovery known, and then this colony of half-castes became the pets of the world. English war ships went to visit them, this time not for vengeance, but to carry them all whereof they stood in need, in loving gifts. French war ships looked in, and, charmed with their inno-cence and simplicity, deigned to give them leave to hoist a Gallic flag, but showed no resentment when the offer was declined. America opened her generous hand. It was a place of pilgrimage; mankind seemed to see

much that it might have been in this outland-
ish folk, without a war, a debt, a slave class,
or a bottle of brandy to boast of, but only
with labour and love. So much had been
omitted, from sheer defect of memory and
knowledge in that poor stranded tar. He had
just tried to make them good, and had left the
rest to take care of itself. Suppose he had
come earlier, and caught the whole race
on their exit from the Ark. How it might
have spoiled history—all the devilment of the
world cleared off, and a new start made with
a germ of good! Well, they multiplied,
with this encouragement, till their numbers
threatened to exceed the capacities of the isle,
when a considerate British Government trans-
ported them to another island, ever so far
superior, and set them up in housekeeping.
They flourished; but the new island was the
great world, and the gentler spirits among
them sighed for their worldlet once more. So
these came back to it; and their children and
children's children are here, in the old peace
and beauty of life, to this day.

CHAPTER VII.

SETTLING DOWN.

So much I remember of my reading. and I slowly bring it back to life, with much help in concentration from one of the rafters of yellow wood with which my chamber is roofed. I am steadily gazing at the rafter, as I have been any time this hour past, when I hear a knock at the door, give the familiar pass-word, and receive Victoria's unembarrassed 'Good-morning' as she walks majestically in, and takes a seat on the edge of the bed. I watched her savage cheek for the trace of a blush, but there was none. I hope she did not watch mine.

'Must we call you " Lord "?' she inquired, with grave politeness. 'Father says we ought, but I thought I would ask you first.'

I set her mind at rest on this point, and

then she became herself of yesterday, protecting and calm.

'I came to call you. How long have you been awake? Did you sleep well?' So many questions, one might say, out of an Ollendorff-an First Course in the language of the island.

'Delightfully,' I replied. 'I hope I have not kept breakfast waiting.' (Exercise No. 2.)

'Oh, we have had breakfast long ago,' said Victoria, now beginning real talk, 'and they have all gone to work; but I stayed at home to look after you.'

'What kind of work?'

'Well, work in the plantations—how do you suppose we get our yams?'

'What else?'

'Listen'—and I heard a muffled sound of beating from the back of the house. I had heard it before, but it had passed unnoticed— 'Can't you guess what they are doing there?'

'Not in the least.'

'They are making cloth, tappa cloth. See, here is some of it;' and she showed me the snowy counterpane of my bed. 'We make it from the bark of a tree. I'll show you, by-

and-by. We like English cloth better, though,
when we can get it.   I always dress in English
cloth.'

'So you have done no work to-day, Victoria, all because of me.'

'Oh yes, I have.   I have cooked your
breakfast, and caught it too.   Do you like
fish?'

'What fish?'

'Squid.'

'I hope I do,' I said fervently—'I am
sure I do.'

'Such fun!   I had to go in three times for
him, and was washed off twice.'

'I don't quite understand.'

'In the surf, you know.   They cling to
the rocks; and you have to catch them before
the sea comes back and catches you.'

I remembered my dismal attempt to rule
the waves the night before last, and was
silent with humiliation.

She must have read my thoughts with
her clear eye.   'Oh, none of *you* can swim;
and no wonder—you have such nice ships to
swim for you.   I must give you a few lessons.
We will go right round the island—I will look

after you. But not till you are stronger. Are you strong to-day?' asked Victoria, with the tenderest solicitude, looking down on me as on a babe in its cot.

Upon my word, I thought she was going to offer to dress me. 'As a lion,' I returned, determined to resist this last indignity to the death.

'Well, make haste, and get up,' said Victoria, and she rose and walked out—no better enlightened as to the proprieties, I am afraid, than when she came in.

I was soon in the next room; and for some minutes I had it to myself. This gave me time to look round. It was a long chamber, with windows on one of the longer sides, or rather unglazed openings that might be closed with a shutter. On the opposite side were two beds in recesses facing the light, and screened by sliding panels that made each recess a tiny bed-chamber. Port-holes in the wall above the beds would admit light when the panels were closed. They were not closed now; and the beds, with their coverlets of spotless tappa, formed no insignificant part of the furniture. It appeared to be the great common room of the house, serving all purposes by turns. My breakfast things, spread on a white cloth, stood on the table. There was a large clothes press in one corner, of home make, I should say, but still the work of a craftsman. An old-fashioned writing-desk, in another corner, was evidently from Europe. Floor, walls, and ceiling were of the yellow wood already noticed. There was no fireplace; but a well-stored bookcase hung over what might have been the mantel. In other respects, the place was like a cabinet of curiosities. There were articles of use or ornament that must have come out of the old scuttled ship, with others that were, as clearly, recent gifts from Europe. Some of the gifts were useful; a few would have been purely ornamental, even in the boudoir of a duchess. There was a good timepiece, side by side with a machine for moistening postage stamps. A copper tea-kettle divided the honours of a little sideboard with a miniature chest of drawers, in morocco leather, for the storage of cash— labelled 'Gold,' 'Silver,' 'Notes,' in letters richly embossed. A huge shoehorn in ivory, tapering to a button hook in polished steel, hung against the wall, near an old-fashioned native club. Kind-hearted people at home seemed to have had happy thoughts about the Pitcairn plunders while walking down Bond Srteet, and to have rushed into the first fancy-shop, and bought the first thing that came to hand. The islanders were none the worse for it; they had received these gifts as so much European fetich, and reverently laid them by, without attempting to discover their use.

I was still enjoying this strange feast of the eye, when the Ancient of yesterday, the Governor of the Island, came in. He was between fifty and sixty, tall, straight, and strong, and, in many points of look and manner, a strange survival of the old-fashioned man-of-war's man, though he might never have trod a vessel's deck. He was dressed like a seaman, in blue pilot cloth with brass buttons, that must have come from England. He had the inheritance of a pigtail and side locks, in his way of trimming his hair. He was no swarthier than an English tar who has seen service, in spite of his cross of

native blood. He had softer manners, however, than one would look for in his great
original. Yet, to say the best for him, he
came somewhat short of the common conception of a Governor. His face had something
of the grave beauty of Victoria's, without
any trace of its spiritual charm,

—'Hope you are better, sir,' said his Excellency, laying his hat on the writing-desk.
and holding out his hand. One thing especially charmed me in him. as, afterwards, in all
of them. He was as free as a Spanish peasant
from all subservience of manner born of a
sense of difference in social grade. None of
them seemed to know their station, although.
strangely enough, this implied no ignorance
of their Catechism. The secret of my unfortunate position at home, as revealed by
the visiting card, made me an object of
curiosity, but not in the least of deference,
still less, if possible, of ill will. They seemed
to feel without explanation—what I was at
first so anxious to tell them—that it was no
fault of mine.

After compliments, he gave me his history,
in reply to my eager questions. He was the

grandson of an English mutineer; and both his father and mother were of mixed English and native blood. So, too, was his wife—now dead. Victoria was his only child. The very mention of her, I could see, brought a faint glow of pride to his bronzed cheek; and when she came in, bearing a smoking dish for my breakfast, he embraced her as lovingly as though they had not met for months.

' Be careful, father, or you'll upset the bird,' said the girl, as she laid a baked fowl on the table, which was quite a master-piece as a colour study in luscious browns. It took three journeys to complete her preparations; and then I was invited to sit down to the most deliciously novel repast ever spread before me—grey mullet, and the mysterious squid, now turning out to be the more familiar cuttle-fish, to take off the sharper edge of appetite; the baked bird, with yams, roasted breadfruit, and plantain cake to follow; bananas, oranges, and cocoa-nuts for dessert. The liquors, I am bound to say, were a failure. I was offered water with the fish, and cocoa-nut milk with the bird; and, I suppose, my passing spasm of pain caught Victoria's eye.

'I knew he would never like it,' she said
to her father, 'I must make him some tea,
this minute,' and she flew outside once
more.

I followed, with a bunch of bananas in my
hand, to entreat her not to execute her kindly
intention, and then I discovered that the
kitchen was in the open air. It was the old
Otaheite oven, described by Cook—heated
stones in a hole in the ground, the food laid
on them, and covered with more heated stones,
which, in their turn, were covered with leaves
and cleanly rubbish to keep out every particle
of cold. Half an hour in this bath of hot air
cooks a fowl to perfection. Other things were
new and strange to me. The houses stood
about a yard above the soil on huge sleepers
of stone, and these sleepers, again, were laid
on low terraces of earth, for further security
against damp. Each house was surrounded
by its own plot—a garden in front, and in the
rear a miniature farm-yard, and offices, including the oven, and a shed for the making
of cloth. The roofs were thatched with
leaves, and most of the dwellings had an
upper floor.

CHAPTER VIII.

GOVERNMENT, ARTS, AND LAWS.

VICTORIA goes afield, and I return to the house, to smoke with the Ancient, and to interview him on government, arts, and laws. This is what I learn.

Our population, men, women and children, is less than one hundred souls.

Our arts—well, we till the soil, as aforesaid, but in our own way. The plough and the windmill were unknown to us a few years ago. We breed a little stock, and we exchange wool and tallow for flour and biscuit, with passing ships. When a ship comes to us, we grow wild with joy, and it is fête day throughout the island.

We get most things in this way, and our latest transaction in barter was for slate pencils and files, of which we stood much in need. The school was reduced to chalk and the blackboard. For a long time, we were greatly at a loss for wedding rings ; and the one ring on the Island had to be lent for each successive ceremony. This want is now supplied.

Coin is a curiosity : we have but two sovereigns, a dozen half-crowns, with a choice assortment of minor pieces, and one fourpenny bit. This last stands under an inverted tumbler, which constitutes our nearest approach to a numismatic museum. The collection might increase, if only the ladies could consent to part with their jewelry, for our few English coins are worn as ornaments. There are American dollars in greater plenty, but the currency is chiefly in potatoes.

We think of raising cotton, which would thrive very well in this latitude, and it is quite possible that, in a few years, we may be no longer dependent on Europe for shirts. It would add much to our sense of dignity, and, beside, would tend to make us more self-supporting, in the event of complications with a foreign power.

We have no navy to speak of, but there is a first-rate whale boat. The steersman of the whale boat is also Magistrate, or Governor of the Island—my host. There is precedent for it: Pitt, I believe, was First Lord of the Treasury and Chancellor of the Exchequer, at the same time. The Governor is elected annually, by universal suffrage of both sexes.

O that Governor!

He has just laid down his pipe, to fish the Revised Statutes out of the pocket of his pilot coat. 'We make 'em as we want 'em,' he says simply, 'but I hope we shall soon want no more. There's quite enough already, to my mind.

'You see, sir, the first is a "Law Respecting the Magistrate" (that's me, for the present). He's to carry out the laws, and when there's any complaint to call the people together and hear both sides. Everyone is to treat him with respect. But they all do, you know, without that,' his Excellency was pleased to add.

'Then there's a "Law Regarding the School." All children to go; or to pay, whether they go or not. Fee, a barrel of Irish potatoes a year, or thereabouts.'

'A barrel of Irish potatoes, you see, in

our currency, stands for twelve shillings, and the school fee is a shilling a month. A barrel of sweet potatoes is only eight shillings. Three good bunches of plantains make four shillings, and so on.

'On the 1st of January we visit landmarks, first thing after the election, and see they are all right.

'Then there's a law about drinks, sir—as I dare say you know. No strong liquor on the Island, except for physic. You see, we gave liquor a trial when our people first came here, and the man that invented it went funny, and jumped into the sea. It seemed to bring bad luck, so we gave it up.

'Now we come to our great difficulty,' and he proceeded to read aloud another chapter of the statutes headed, 'Laws for Cats.' 'Cats, you must know, sir, are very useful in keeping down rats, but our young people will sometimes shoot them for sport, so we've been obliged to pass a very severe law, our severest, I may say. There's a heavy fine for killing a cat, half of it to go to the informer. For all that, it's no easy matter to settle these cases. Sometimes people say the cat came to kill their fowls; and what are you to do then? It is a difficult case for a magistrate. I always say this—was the cat caught killing the bird; or was it merely a suspicion? If you can't produce your dead bird, then down with your potatoes! There's another way; you may pay your fine in rats killed by yourself. Three hundred is the price of a cat's life; we try to be fair all round.

'Take fowls again; if a fowl trespasses in your garden, you may shoot it, and the owner must return you your charge of powder and shot. That's the law as it stands in the book, but nowadays you generally send back the bird, and say no more about it. We are all neighbours, you know.

'There's another thing,' continued his Excellency, pursuing his commentary on the code, 'You mustn't carve on trees. Who wants to carve on trees? you may say. Well, the young people, when they are a-courting. But it ruins the timber. We've had no end of trouble with that law. As you walk about the Island, sir, you'll come upon true lovers' knots, and such like, in the most out of the

way places. You mustn't be startled by 'em,
and think it's savages ; it's just sweethearts,
neither more or less. Where we can't tell
which pair was walking there, I draws 'em
all up in line, and asks who did it, straight
out. Oh, you have to look sharp after things
here, I do assure you. Our people are not
so wicked, but they get careless sometimes.
Who'd ever think, now, that we want a " Law
for the Public Anvil "? but we do.' And he
read aloud,

' " Any person taking the public anvil and
public sledge-hammer from the blacksmith's
shop is to take it back after he has done with
it ; and, in case the anvil and sledge-hammer
should get lost, by his neglecting to take it
back, he is to get another anvil and sledge-
hammer, and pay a fine of four shillings "—
potatoes, you know.

' You've got a good many more laws in
Europe, I've heard say,' he observed, as he
closed his book, and restored the entire code
of Pitcairn to his breast pocket.

' You have not been misinformed,' I replied. ' But tell me—have you any machinery

of appeal from the decisions of the Court of
First Instance ? '

'Well,' he said, 'if they don't like what I
tell 'em, it goes before a jury.'

'And if they don't like that any better ? '

'Then we hold over till the next British
man-o'-war touches, and the captain decides.
We've got an appeal waiting now—a cat
case. None of us can get to the rights
of it, so we must wait : but the parties are
friendly enough, meanwhile.'

'Have you ever carried a case to the House
of Lords ? '

'We shouldn't like to trouble you, sir,
thank you, all the same.'

CHAPTER IX.

NURSE.

VICTORIA is my nurse. There is no doubt of it: I am in her charge. She governs all my goings out, and my comings in, and is told off, I think, to see that I do not drown myself, or fall off the rocks. For a few days I see next to nothing of the others. They are gone out to work long before I get up, and I catch mere glimpses of them in our walks afield. They come up in the evening, to look at me through the windows, but Victoria heads them off, with a promise to produce me on Sunday. I am supposed to be convalescent in the meanwhile. I am quite content, and I sham.

The housewives, of course, see me, as I walk through the village. They have all kissed me, nobody objecting, I least of all. I am the best of friends with the children, and

these always call me 'Lord.' Victoria calls
me by my Christian name.

She wakes me in the morning, feeds me
as aforesaid, then takes me for an airing, perhaps to St. Paul's Point, a thousand feet high,
which affords a fine bird's-eye view of infini-
tude. When the ascent becomes unusually
steep, she grasps me by the arm, and pushes
me up. It is useless to try to shake her off;
I need her as much in that country as Gul-
liver needed Glumdalclitch elsewhere. The
goats can hardly follow us sometimes. Her
education has been neglected in the matter
of nerves; she stands on perpendicular summits, and coils her hair; she drops on ledges
of rock less than a yard wide, to rescue a
stray kid, and walks to and fro on them with
a certitude that precludes courage. Never
have I felt so small. There is nothing to keep
up the fiction of knightly service, not a fan to
hold, a carriage door to open, a wrap to arrange. So I make no more pretence of homage to the sex than any other infant in charge.
Fractiousness, on the contrary, is rather my
cast of mind ; if anything, I am a troublesome
child.

In all things she is a model nurse, and especially in this, that she teaches me to tell the truth. I had no idea of what truthfulness might mean, till I came here. Victoria never says the thing that is not, and she sometimes misses the most tempting effects of humour, in consequence. Her yea is yea, her nay, nay. So, it seems, the primitive founder from Wapping understood his charge under the Writ. Whatever is she states as it is, and this mere habit often gives her talk the charm of classic prose. The Ancient, as we have seen, in his love-knot cases, supplies the want of a detective police by public confession. I praised her once for this virtue; she said I had strange ideas.

It kills coquetry, though. 'I don't think you care for me one bit, Victoria,' I said one day. 'Why should I care for you?' I, of course, expected on her part, as the next move in the game. All the best treatises lay this down as the appropriate answer. But Victoria simply played the native gambit. 'I am sure I do: I like you very much. How stupid of me never to think of telling you! So does father too.' I threw a stone at a goat, by way of changing the subject, and Victoria redoubled her attentions all the way home. I could only throw more stones at the goats. Shooting, alas! was out of the question : all the live things were stock, and they had no stock to spare.

She tells me stories, like the best of nurses, stories of that unregenerate early time, when evil was killing itself out of the island, and the Devil stinging himself to death with the fork of his own tail. There is a story of an awful night, which I often ask for. All the native men had risen on all the English, and left but one of them alive, the future law-giver, and him half dead. Then, when darkness fell, the native women stole on the sleeping murderers, and finished them. This was the last massacre ; the Devil was dead in Pitcairn. The scene is always with me, as the background of the picture of to-day. Here the sweet benignant maids and wives, the sunshine and the peace ; there the dusky furies they sprang from, stealing forth in the night to the deed of blood. Love redeemed, if it did not justify; and ah, how these Southern women possess that finest of the arts! At Tahiti—it is another of Victoria's stories—when the avenging war ship came out to fetch the mutineers home to be hanged, one of them was torn from the side of Peggy, his native wife, who held an infant at her breast. He lay heavily ironed on deck, when Peggy climbed the side, infant and all, from a canoe—as it was thought, only to say a discreet good-bye. But Peggy behaved without discretion, throwing herself on the poor manacled wretch, hugging his very fetters, to get a little nearer the father of her baby, and sobbing the most heart-breaking things to him in the *patois* of her isle. He turned, and begged she might be led away, as though he were already tasting something sharper than death. Led away she was, and sent back in her canoe, and she made such haste to die of a broken heart that she was at peace long before he went down in his irons in the storm that nearly destroyed the whole ship's company, captives and all, on the homeward voyage.

Once, it might have been a ghost story. I am walking with Victoria at night, through a deep gorge, to show her the scene of my disaster in the landing. A high ridge bounds

the valley; and chancing to raise her eyes to
it, the girl suddenly utters a cry of terror,
and clings all trembling to me. 'Tell me
what it is—I cannot look at it.' Then, as
suddenly, she flings herself away from me,
cowering, and will not be touched; and, with
hands clasped, utters more cries of mystery,
in which I am not concerned. 'Oh !—if !
—speak to me, only ! come to me ! I have
not forgotten, I have not done wrong.' There
is certainly something stirring up there, in the
green moonlight, but Victoria will in nowise
let me obey her order to find out what it is,
but draws me back into the shadow of the
gorge, and insists on our hurrying home.
Amiable and harmless ghost, the girl is mute
about thee, and I am fain to be content with
thy biography from the Ancient's lips. The
Ridge is haunted by the phantom of a
murdered chief, another of the victims of that
old wild time. The news of our adventure
spreads through the settlement, and no one
peeps in at the windows that night.

She takes me for walks, too, the cun-
ningest. There is a wild cave at the western
end, where one of the mutineers, ever haunted

by the dread of that avenging ship, used to entrench himself against possible attempts at capture that were never made. He would sit there whole summer days, his eye on a narrow rim of rock that led to his cavern, and that one man might, with ease, have kept inviolate against a hundred. He was provisioned and stored for a long siege, and a hard fight; and as he sat watching through the long hours, no doubt he had his thoughts. The eastern end has its cave too, another sanctuary, but of far-off aboriginal man, who carved sun, moon and stars on its walls, and then retired into eternal oblivion and the night of things. The vanished one's modest avoidance of publicity could not fail to be remarked, in spite of him. He had found, or made, his cavern, in the face of a wall of rock that rose some six hundred feet sheer from the foaming sea. A few feet from the summit, there was a ledge just wide enough to support a man, and this was the pathway to his chapel of little ease.

At our first visit, Victoria dropped on the ledge with the mingled lightness and precision of fall of a weighted feather, forbidding me to follow, on pain of death. I did follow, in spite of the prohibition, whereupon she stood stock still on the ledge, till I could recover touch of her, and then burst into tears. The tears saved me, for I was beginning to look down the wall into the surf, and that way self-murder lay. They made me look up at Victoria, though I could not see her face. She recovered herself in a moment. 'Now you will shut your eyes,' she said, 'lay both hands on my shoulders, and walk straight on after me.' So we reached the cave, when she turned and faced me, and began to cry once more. 'How am I to get you back? Why, not all *our* people can walk here—only the youngest!   I will never take you out again, *never*; I mean, *perhaps* I never will.' I examined the curiosities of the cave meanwhile, and assumed a silent, remorseful air. Then came the return journey. 'Try to forget all about the scolding,' said Victoria, 'I take it back—for the present—and do just as you did before.' It was done; and I declare the indefinable charm of companionship with her in peril was a sufficient antidote to fear. 'Now,' she said, when we reached the end of the pathway, 'keep your eyes shut, and hold on to this till I come to you.' And she guided my hand to a small projection, and scrambled, by what I afterwards found was an almost perpendicular facet, to the top of the rock. In a few seconds, something soft touched my face; it was a long woollen girdle, that Victoria sometimes wore, and she had lowered it to my aid. I, too, reached the level at last. 'I shall not speak to you for some time,' she said, resuming the quarrel, and she stalked on ahead, I meekly following without a word. She turned as we reached the path leading to the settlement. 'Do you unfeignedly repent?' When she was most serious she often talked the English of the Church Service, and without the faintest sense of incongruity. 'Victoria, I can hardly find words—' 'Very well, then: I forgive you from my heart, though, you know, I am not obliged to forgive you till sundown. But it would be a pity to waste an afternoon.'

We finished the day in great amity, under the shade of a banyan tree, whither we retired for consultation on a matter that gave Victoria some perplexity of spirit. She had lately bought a Milton from a passing ship—with her own savings in potatoes—and had read it through so often that she knew long passages by heart. The work had left in her mind an impression of unfairness in the treatment of Satan, and she was most anxious to submit this difficulty to the judgment of a friend. I was at first disposed to make light of it, but I soon saw that Victoria took it very seriously indeed. They had but few books ; each book went the round of the settlement; and it was taken in most edifying good faith, as a report from that visionary outer world, that unexplored planet, whose laws, customs, institutions, ways of being and doing were such a mystery to the worldlet of the rock. The hero of the latest volume to hand, novel, history or poem, no matter what its date, was always the personage of the day at Pitcairn. His difficulties were the living issues in politics, morals, and the art of life.

'I am going to say something about it at the meeting to-morrow night; but I thought I should like to speak to you first. I do not think he was properly treated, though Mr. John Milton seems to have no pity for him.

and he ought to know. Yet I cannot think it. I could hardly sleep at all, last night; it troubled me so.'

'Well, Victoria, I suppose he staked his stake, and lost, and had to put up with the consequences ; that is all I see.'

'Yes, but perhaps if they had only been kinder to him, he might have repented. He was very proud. you know, and there was no one to soothe him. I think Gabriel was very haughty and hard with him, and Zephon quite disrespectful, considering his place. Do you always approve of Gabriel?' she asked, with much earnestness, and looking me straight in the eyes, as though our friendship depended on the answer. 'Surely,' she said, with rising warmth, ' you would never stand up for that speech at the end of the fourth book. Rulers should not be so high and distant, just clearing their throats, and giving their commands, as though all others were servants. Suppose father ruled like that—who would obey the laws? I know Satan felt it. It is a pity he had no good female angel to take care of him —only there is no marrying, nor giving in marriage there : so they say,' and she sighed.

'People may meet again, though, without marrying,' she said after a pause, and with her eyes fixed on the vacancy of sea and sky. 'Thank God for that! But oh what meetings, if they have not been true!' She seemed to have forgotten Satan for a moment, I thought, but I soon brought her back to the case before the court.

'There was an attempt to bring feminine influence to bear on him, I believe, but it hardly turned out well.'

'When? where? Mr. John Milton says nothing about it.'

'No, that comes from another reporter, a Frenchman. It did not answer. A pitying angel left Paradise, to come and speak comfort to him, as he lay writhing on his hot bed. She was fearful, though compassionate, and she meant always to keep out of arm's length. But her pity drew her too near, all the same, and he clutched her, and dragged her down. So runs the tale.'

'I don't believe a word of it,' said Victoria firmly, 'I think he never had a chance. I shall say so at the meeting; and you back me up.'

CHAPTER X.

SUNDAY.

I WAS produced on Sunday before the whole
settlement; more strictly speaking, they produced themselves before me. The villagers
were in the village, for the first time, at my
hour of rising. There was an absolute cessa-
tion from labour, but there was hardly rest.
They were in a flutter of joyous excitement,
and ran from cottage to cottage, as though
they were spreading good news. Yet there
was no news, for who could need telling that
it was Sunday, and that the sky was blue?
For that matter, they needed no excuse to
make free of each other's houses. Property
in their own roofs seemed the merest accident
among them. One man's arm-chair was
another man's arm-chair. They walked in
and out, by the open doors—often into unguarded dwellings, when the owners were on

a visit elsewhere—read the books, smelt the
flowers, touched the harmonium, if they could,
or cared, and came away. When you sought
a man, you went into the nearest cottage;
you never thought of going first to his own,
unless it lay in your path. There was more
of this curious house to house visiting to-day,
because there was more time for it, and because there was a greater intensity of childlike
happiness in movement and communion—that
was all.

There seemed to be much borrowing and
lending of the Sabbath finery of cleanliness.
If you had no better coat for the day, why,
your neighbour might have one to spare, and
you asked him for it. Victoria lent two loose
gowns, a kind of *robe de chambre* worn on
state occasions over the scanty costume of the
women. At the same time, she went into a
neighbour's garden, and helped herself freely
to flowers for her hair, our own stock having
suffered from the movements of some four-
footed intruder during the night. If Proud-
hon had lived here, he would have written
' property is vanity,' the innermost truth.
Victoria was very smart—a new ribbon for

the navy button, beside the blossoms inwoven with her shining locks.

The church was a hut. I have seen St. Peter's, too, yet I give this one the preference for majesty, taking its surroundings into account. For St. Peter's, as the best thing in its quarter, all else meaner, leads nowhere beyond itself, while this island fane, backed first by a stately tropic grove, then by a towering cone of mountain, then by the clouds, carried the eye from height to height of beauty and of wonder, right up to Heaven.

We were rather late, and it was all the better, for now I could take in the whole population of the island at a glance. They were mostly of superb physique, men and women, and Victoria was but one finest example of them. Reuben, the young giant, who had helped me on the day of landing, was another. Among the women, however, some foolish hat, or trailing skirt, of civilisation here and there departed from the classic simplicity of Victoria's dress. Most of the men wore shoes, in honour of the day ; a few, like the Ancient, long trousers, instead of the loose knee-breeches of their working suits.

Trousers seemed to be a sign of authority, or of the beginning of years. The priest, or ministrant, wore them, and indeed he might have been entitled to wear two pairs, for, 1 think, he was schoolmaster as well. The types varied from Victoria's front of Western Europe to almost pure Tahiti, but always they had their point of unity in the large soft eyes.

For the service, never had I seen such fervour, such passion of prayer and praise! It was the Church of England form, I believe, but form of any kind was hardly to be recognised in the melting heat of their zeal. The poor old Litany seemed like a veritable audience at the throne of God. The Commandments came as His voice from our own mountain, thundering from the summit of the cone. Our hymns soared after Him to the very farthest heaven as He retired. One boy's note, I think, must have got there first, so clear was it, so clean and pure and true, with nought of earth to keep it from the skies. It was a living faith, no mere specimen of what once had lived, dried for keeping, and not even dried in the sun. Here were the true Primitives, the joyous band of Galilean vagabonds, exulting in that new conception of the brother-hood of man whose secret we have for ever lost. Solemnity, as we understand it, seemed far from them ; devoutness was swallowed up in joy. Often they laid their hands affection-ately on each other's shoulders as they sang : once I saw two children kiss after a prayer.

I had been completely ignored during the service, but, when it was over, my turn came. As we trooped back towards the village, I was the centre of a questioning crowd. I had come from England—that was enough, for England is their great archetype of power, wisdom, and beauty of life. Needless to say they have not seen it ; I mean, of course, that circumstance has bound them to their rock. All that they know as best comes from England, from the great war ship, which they regard with almost the wonder of Indians, down to the harmonium in the cottage. It is not much to know, but a generous imagina-tion easily does the rest. England has been good to them : England, then, is goodness. She is visibly strong : then she is strength. She has sent them Bibles ; ah ! she must be the Word made Flesh.

So it was one long bewildering inquisition. Would I tell them of the great churches, the great wonders manifold of that far-off Isle of the Saints? What of the rulers and statesmen, of the bishops, those captains of captains of the thousands of God, of the choirs of the faithful—five thousand strong, as they had heard—hymning Handel under a crystal dome? They seemed to see human life not at all as a mere struggle, but as a great race for a crown of virtue, in which Britain was first, and their poor island so decidedly nowhere that she could afford to sink rivalry in unqualified admiration. I winced, and winced, and winced again.

'We are but poor things here, and we know it,' said the schoolmaster.

'You will improve,' I said kindly.

'Well, sir, we are always ready to learn; perhaps you would like to take a service yourself next Sunday? You are not in orders, but you have heard the Archbishop of Canterbury, I dare say.'

'No, only a bishop now and then.'

'Oh, what opportunities!' said Victoria sadly. 'We once had a navy-chaplain here, but it was four years ago. Though, of course, that is no excuse for our not being better than we are.'

'They say he has fifteen thousand a year to spend on the poor,' said the schoolmaster, returning to the Primate.

' Yes, he has fifteen thousand a year.'

' How much would that be in potatoes, let's see?' murmured Reuben, and he withdrew for an operation in mental arithmetic.

' I've heard of a lady who has made fifty thousand people happy, all by herself,' said one of the women. ' She's a baroness.'

' And that's not the highest,' said another, ' there's duchesses who must be richer. Oh, what a country for the poor ! '

' It's the big churches I'm thinking of,' observed the schoolmaster. ' Why, there's one that holds six thousand people. Six thousand people, twice a day! Think of the spread of it ! '

' Them's the things I want to see,' said Reuben, returning, not unoppressed, I thought, by his weight of potatoes, ' the big things— St. Paul's, the Railway.'

' You should use the plural form, Reuben,' urged the schoolmaster gently, ' the railways.

There are dozens of them. Why, there are
three great lines running to Birmingham! I've
got a map of it.'

' And how about the Parliament ? ' struck
in the Ancient, pre-occupied, and not un-
naturally, with the question of legislation.
·'Over a thousand people to make the laws ; and
at it day and night, too ! The moment anything goes wrong anywhere, there they are,
waiting on the premises, as you may say, to
put it right. We've nothing like that here.
Not that we want it either; I only make the
remark.'

This touching disposition to take us in good
faith had no limits. In their quaint conception of our corporate life, all things existed
to that great end of the crown of virtue.
Nothing was merely neutral or indifferent.
To talk of making people virtuous by Act of
Parliament would, for them, have had none
of the significance of a sneer. What else
were Acts of Parliament for ? So, churches
were to promote brotherhood and love, with
no reserves for a Pickwickian sense ; armies,
to suppress the wicked. Rank and riches,
as we have just seen, were mere equivalents

for more opportunity; if a baroness made fifty thousand people happy, what might not a duchess do? The islanders simply multiplied our means by their own yearnings, and the product was a colossal sum in good. Everything seemed to count; from a question the Ancient put to me as to the number of cabs and omnibuses in the British capital, I more than suspect that these, too, contributed to his grand total. The drivers were obliging persons whose chief concern was to give tired Righteousness a lift.

'I want to see St. Paul's and the railways,' murmured Reuben again, in an amended version, as he wandered away from the group.

Victoria's wistful gaze went after him: 'Poor fellow!'

'Is anything the matter with him, Victoria?'

'Yes, but he daren't tell anyone but me; he wants to go.'

'To go where?'

'Out there,' she said, with a gesture that was meant to indicate the world at large. 'He wants to see it all; he can never rest here. These things our people talk about with strangers trouble him. He's venturous; he must see and know. He was always like that: he dived two fathoms lower than any-one else—off the Point, and brought up a watch from the old ship. No one can follow him on the rocks. He discovered an island once—over there. I went to see it: I'll take you one day. Now it's England. He can never rest here. But, oh! how I dread it! and, besides, you know, they will never let him go.'

'Did he find so much in the first island. then, that he longs to try the other?'

'No; only some dry bones in a cave. But England will be different, of course.'

They prayed and praised, in the exultant fashion of the morning, all day long—with due intervals for refreshment. There were five services, I think, big and little. If there were not six, it was only because this Sunday did not happen to fall on the longest day.

'I hope it is because we love God,' said Victoria, 'but I think it is just as much be-cause we love one another. Or perhaps it is to bring Him nearer, so that we may love Him like the rest. He must not be too far off. I think that is why some of the poor wild people we read of take so long to convert. You must show them something, and let them feel the strong arm, and see the face of human love. They always want to worship the missionary first. Why not let them ; and then pass it on, when they get stronger ? Do you know, in spite of all my advantages, I could sometimes just fall down and say my prayers to a child, to things even—a rose-tree ? It's the old wickedness in our blood, I suppose. But mind, don't you dare tell anybody ; I should die of shame !'

I had begged to be excused from attendance at the remaining four services, on the ground that I preferred an open-air rite ; and, on my assurance that this mode of devotion had the sanction of British custom, Victoria had consented to join me. We were wandering, talking, musing in long silences, picking wild-flowers, breathing the balmy air, basking in the warm light.

In one of these reveries I caught a strange gleam in Victoria's eyes. 'Tell me about the blessed Sabbaths in England,' she murmured, placing her hand in mine.

O my England, my England! why cannot I speak of a thing we all must honour so? why, rather, do I pray for strength to keep the secret of thy Sabbaths well? Dread day of the division of classes, weekly vision of the Judgment, in its utter separation of the social sheep and goats, never one flock, alas! at any time, but now so clearly two. In this dark hour of remembrance, I hear the hoarse clappers of thy meeting-houses, vainly fanning the stagnant air in cities of the spiritual dead. I see thy funereal processions of the elect, wending to or from the conventicles, past groups of coster-boys, who wait for the opening of the houses, and expectorate on the pavement in patterns of the dawn of decorative art. It is all before me, the dingy squalor of thy miles of shuttered marts, the crying contrasts of thy Sunday finery, more hurtful to the eye than thy week-day rags! I hear thy muffin-bells in the deep silences, and thy hawkers' wail; and, amid this worst of all spiritual destitution, the destitution of beauty, I ask myself, what is it that we have lost; what is it these little ones have found?

CHAPTER XI.

A SAIL.

I WAS roused next morning by the report of a gun, followed by a strange commotion in the village. I had barely time to dress, and join the Ancient in the sitting-room, when a man ran in, breathless, to announce a ship off the Point, and a Queen's ship.

A Queen's ship! No wonder the village was astir. A ship that might fly the Royal Standard, a ship that was English authority and English might! No work in the Island this day!

The Ancient put on his Sunday coat, and quietly took command. ' How lucky the landing is easy this morning! Jonah, hurry off to the Point, with the white flag, and signal their cutter " All right! " Quintal, you go down to the landing, and see them over the breakers.   Now, folks, who's to take them in?'

It was a call to public meeting on the question of the entertainment of the officers. The islanders always claimed this privilege of boarding and lodging the Queen's uniform. Half a dozen heads of families at once offered to provide for as many guests. There was a brisk competition for the Captain, who would have fallen to the Governor *ex-officio*, but for my occupancy of the spare bedroom in his Excellency's house. I offered to retire, but my generous hostess would not hear of it.

'I found him, father, and he belongs to me,' said Victoria, in the terms of that earlier claim which had sometimes made me suspect the existence of slavery in the Island. The blood of the free-born ought to have rushed to my face in protest against this attempt to count me as a chattel; but it did not.

The Captain is knocked down to the schoolmaster; the women hurry away to light their ovens; the meeting breaks up. Its dispersed groups, however, form so many sub-committees of reception, for they talk of nothing but the comfort and delight of the public guests.   The only private interest is represented by the two litigants who have the case on appeal from a decision of the Island courts to the supreme tribunal of a British man-of-war.   They are tossing with a parti-coloured bean, to see which shall open the pleadings first.

The Ancient, hurrying down to the landing-place, calls for his whale-boat and his mariners three, and our navy goes forth in mod st pride to meet the Queen's ship. She is close in-shore, the depth of water admitting of a near approach; so, when our Governor boards her, we see all that passes.   His Excellency takes off his hat, and pulls at a forelock that is not there to pull.   No real one has been pulled in that family since the time of George III., but the gesture has survived with them as a sign of respect.   The Captain shakes hands with him, and presents him to his officers, who do the same.   Then they leave the clean white deck, flashing light from its polished brasses, and go below, as though for complimentary refresh-ments.   On their return, the Governor takes charge of the ship's cutter, in which our guests embark. Only a native can dodge the rocks, rocklets, and surf currents of our bay. They wait at the back of the rollers till the look-out man ashore waves his hat; then they give way with a will, and are hurled in, safely, on the crest of the wave.

Two of the officers are old friends of mine. What a little world it is! You would think all were old friends of the islanders, by the warmth of welcome. Men, women and children struggle for a grasp of their hands, and a girl offers flowers to the Captain. He kisses her; his officers kiss the other girls: fathers, brothers, and cousins hurrah approval, and content.

Then we lead them to the schoolhouse, by the steep paths, in joyous procession of old and young. Here the Captain must enter in the Island register the name of his ship, with other particulars, and meet a deputation of the elders, who come to trade. The ship wants water, yams, and potatoes: we want hardware. The terms of exchange are settled according to a written tariff, and the elders depart, to weigh over the commodities on their side. They are poor traders, though:

yams are scarce at the moment, yet they ask no higher price for them; nor can I make them understand that to do so would be to seek an honest gain. 'Is there less steel in the hatchets than there used to be,' they ask, 'that we are to give less in yams?' I remember that the value of a thing is what it will fetch, and I tell them so, but they shake their heads. For the first time, it occurs to me that these people have no natural turn for economic speculation; and that, with all their religion, they may need a missionary of a kind. A certain finer sense is wanting; but no more of this just now.

The guests have, meanwhile, been led to their quarters, the Captain beaming with affability and good nature. He foresees his report to the Lords of the Admiralty on the morals, manners and customs of these inno-cent islanders, with the articles thereon in the daily papers. It is all such a relief after the official landings of the Pacific station, and the French polish of the South American dons, much tarnished by keeping in a torrid clime.

The people are as curious and inquisitive as children. They draw the officers' swords,

run their fingers along the dulled edges, cry
wonder at the damascened blades. Some of
them have never seen the uniform before :
none can ever see it too often. They have
the fullest confidence in the honour of the
wearers ; and they give themselves up to enjoyment, without a thought of harm. All the
rules governing their intercourse with traders
are suspended. The girls go where they
please, with whom they please : every middy,
even, has his feminine aide-de-camp, and local
guide. The Captain is attended by no less
a person than the Ancient himself, though I
think he would prefer to rough it with his
officers. The Ancient treats him with a fine
courtesy, affecting not to be master in his own
domain.

Nor indeed is he master for the time—at
least on the judicial side. The Queen's navy,
as already stated, is our court of final appeal
under the constitution ; and there is that un-
settled case. It is called on the morrow of
the Captain's visit, with the cocoa grove for
the seat of the appellate tribunal. The
Ancient offered the schoolhouse, but the Judge
asked why a clearing in the trees would not

do as well; and his will was law. It is quieter than most halls of justice, for the whispers are lost in the open air. The twitter of the birds overhead is not so troublesome as an usher's cry of 'Silence in Court.' The gentle breeze is hardly an inconvenience, for there are no papers to blow about; and the perfume which it brings from the village gardens would be a distinct improvement to the atmosphere of Lincoln's Inn.

I had never quite understood this case, and no wonder, for it had puzzled all the courts of the Island. A cat had been killed: it opened in that way, clearly enough, but, soon after, the obscurity began. Who killed the cat? Even here there was broad daylight —one Elias McCall. Was he justified in the deed? — Ha! His plea was that the cat had sought the lives of his chickens, and that, after losing several of these in successive midnight raids, he had, at length, sought the life of the cat. The law of the case is perfectly explicit: the cat that slays fowl shall itself be slain. But the proof of murderous outrage must be con-clusive: the cat must be 'positively detected in killing'—the Ancient read the statute from his pocket-book, at the request of the Court. Now, was the circumstantial evidence so strong as to constitute detection within the meaning of the Act? The proprietor of the fledglings, as a truthful man, could say no more than that the cat had been in the habit of taking up her station near his hen-coop in the cool of the evening, and that, on the morrow of every such visit, he had missed one or more birds. He had put two and two together, that was his expression, and finally, his feelings getting the better of him, he had 'let go' at the cat (the Ancient, at this point, bade him remember in whose presence he stood), with the result that his brood thereafter remained intact. On a post-mortem examination, moreover, he had found a small feather clinging to the fur. Pressed by the other side, he was bound in honour to admit that he had never seen the cat looking at the hen-coop—on the contrary, her head was usually turned the other way. She often sang to herself, as though pre-occupied; and her movements were so little of a threatening nature that she was washing her face at the very moment of the fatal stroke. It was not denied that there were many other cats in the neighbourhood; it was not denied that the fowls often flew upon the fence where the cat used to sit, nor that they might there have left the stray feather found on her person. With this evidence, the owner of the cat left his case in the hands of the Supreme Court. The courts below had decided against him, the Ancient first, as Chief Magistrate, and then a jury. Now, the Captain of H.M.S. 'Rollo' was asked to give the final award.

That his Honour was troubled was evident by the frequency with which he asked his assessor, the First Lieutenant, to give him a light for his cheroot. The 'positively detected' of the statute was his stumbling-block; we could see that with half an eye.

'Where did you find the feather?' he said at length, 'near the tail end, where the cat might have been sitting?' It was a leading question, but no one seemed to notice the irregularity. 'No, sir,' returned the murderer, 'on her cheek, just under the right whisker.'

'That settles it, I think,' said the Judge; 'she was washing up, after she had eaten the

bird.' ' Yes, that settles it,' echoed the First
Lieutenant. ' That settles it, of course,' said
the ship's surgeon, who, as a mere bystander,
had no business to deliver an opinion on the
matter. ' That settles it,' said the Ancient;
' I never thought of asking the question.'
' That settles it,' said all the villagers present,
including, strange to say, the owner of the cat.
—Judgment of the courts below confirmed.

CHAPTER XII.

THREE DAYS.

BUSINESS over, our pleasures begin. They are to stay only three clear days in all, and we must make the most of them, putting as much into every precious hour as though it were to be our last of joy.

We visit the ship. She invites us to a party, puts on a little bunting for the occasion, and fires a gun. Everybody goes. The Captain is aboard, and makes believe he has never been ashore, shaking hands with us as we climb the side, though he left us but an hour ago. He wears his cocked hat and epaulettes, by special request; his officers, too, have not been sparing of their best. His crew, subdued to the most mealy-mouthed propriety of speech by such glimpses as they have had of the Island life, entertain us with a concert. It is the forecastle fiddle and accordion, with the repertory of the cockney music-halls. This last seems to lose vitality on our pure uplands, and to gasp for the breath of its native fen. Our good folk listen to ' Blow me up an apple-tree,' or ' Did 'em do it, did 'em, did 'em did 'em do ? ' believing it must be right, because it is English, yet beginning to doubt—not us, however, but themselves, beautiful first form of the doubt of candid souls ! Some of the songs are too far away from them for even the glimmerings of comprehension—the humour of the mere sordidness of life. ' Penny paper-collar Joe.'—Well, they wear no collars ; consequently, they make no paper imitations ; consequently, these cost neither a penny nor a pound. For the same reason, ' O father, dear father, the brokers are in !' leaves them stone-cold. ' What are the brokers ?' whispers Victoria to me. How curious to have to expound these elementary things ! ' Hush, Victoria, not now—when they are gone— it would take all day. Listen to the ballads of the people.' Next it is a fantasia of punning effects :

> A sloth is not an idol ;
> A bride can't wear a bridle,
> Though surely by the (h)altar she is led ;
> Sixpence is not a tanner ;
> A bridegroom's not a banner,
> Though the banns he will put up before he's wed.

I tremble : a little more, and the whole secret will be out, of the murk of mind in which so many of our brethren live, while Lord Tennyson is at the tailor's about his ermine, and dilettantism attends its monthly meeting of the Browning Society, and leaves them in their pen. A little more, and they may suspect that beauty and taste are all grown for Mayfair by the Jews, just like the big pine apples, and that the poet himself is but one more market gardener for the rich. This lyre of the slums threatens to kill the whole pageant ; these sewer gases seem to tarnish the gold lace on the Captain's hat.

'How nice it must be to have your English sense of humour,' says Victoria, ' and to be able to enjoy all these funny things!'

Saved ! Once more they have taken the blame upon themselves.

We wander over the ship ; admire the cutlasses in their racks ; fit our heads in the muzzle of a big gun, gravely waiting our turn in file, under the orders of a corporal ; eat cake in the Captain's cabin, refuse wine ; see everything, ask foolish questions everywhere. Never-to-be-forgotten day ! A tar dances a hornpipe for us ; three of our girls dance the rhythmic dance of Tahiti for the tars. The Captain asks questions about it, and takes notes, always in view of that report to the Lords of the Admiralty. Some of us are photographed—no, it is getting too maddeningly gay ! The Ancient looks grave, and gives the signal for departure. The cutters are lowered ; the little whaler takes its freight again ; the boats dance us home in the dusk. It is not all over yet ; they send up a rocket and a blue light, to say ' Good-night,' as we step ashore. Never-to-be-forgotten day !

And there are more such days to come— days when it is our turn, once more, to do the honours. Our girls take the distinguished visitors over the Island—to the cave of the Carvings, the cave of the Watcher, the Point —tending them carefully on ledge and summit and declivity, as my nurse tended me. They try to do without such guidance,

and come to grief over it, figuring as meanly
as the sinking Cæsar crying for help. The
water sports are just as disheartening. What
stoutest man among us will follow this sea-
nymph, in her sea toilette, plunging into
the breakers with a plank in her arms,
diving and ducking till she comes to the far
side of the hugest wave, then lying flat on
the curling crest, and rolling in with it, till
it breaks in thunder on the rocks? Always,
after the explosion, you look for a mangled
body, and you find only a laughing Venus,
rising whole and perfect from the foam.

Nature herself smiles benignly on the
festival, and contributes to it with great sun-
sets that touch the summits of grove and
mountain with indescribable beauty, and harmonise into perfect peacefulness of association
even the tumult of the breakers in their everlasting strife with the shore. There are fish-
ings by torchlight, later on, in the intense
shadow of the rocks; above us, the corus-
cating wall of rock towering to the moonlit heaven; below, the deep, deep water, all
black and horrible beyond our tiny circle of
flame. The cod flock to the light, like their

betters, and get speared with a five-pronged
fork for their pains. The girls, who are deftest
at the exercise, look not unlike Britannia on the
halfpenny, as they sit at ease with their forks,
waiting their turn. Now, we paddle out of
the shadow into the silvered sea, and so ashore
to the green. Then there is another concert
(ours this time), with simple songs of meeting
and of parting, mostly of the schoolmaster's
writing, quired by the voices of virgins, and,
with such rendering—the scene and the hour
also taken into account—pure intuitions of
the deeper significance of life. Impossible to
doubt, after this, that the spirit is to be lord
of the house; that living is the finest of the
fine arts, or nothing; and that such is the
message, delivered through Nature, of the
Unknowable behind the Nature veil.

The Ancient is thoughtful all the while,
thoughtfullest at the hour of the breaking-up
of this great council of the soul, when the
councillors wander away in pairs, and are lost
in the radiant hazes of the night. It is the
last council—to-morrow they go. Our Chief
has led the way to his cottage, and has asked
the Captain to step in on his way home. ‘I

wish you gentlemen might never come here,' he says pleasantly to his guest, ' or, if you come, I wish you might never go away. It is a moment's pastime for some of you, but, one way or other, it lasts some of us a lifetime. " Jack ashore "—I've heard of him from my father's father; but then he goes ashore so often. Our girls never forget—that's their nature. I've known 'em die, sir, of these visits of a Queen's ship. They think it's only a beginning—your youngsters think it too, Captain, while the moon shines—I *know* it's an ending, for ever and ever. They'll never meet again, sir, in this world—although, at this very minute, perhaps, they're a-cutting love-knots all over the place to make believe they will.'

The incidental reference to the love-knots seemed to have set him on a new track of reflection. ' It's a pity to spoil the trees for nothing, all the same,' he murmured, ' and, if you'll excuse the liberty, I think I'll just have a look round.'

He stole out to watch the public property; and, by his orders, no doubt. Victoria, who had lingered in the garden, came in to enter-

tain the guest. Yet Victoria said not a word.
She had been unlike her old self all the time
of their stay ; she had become pensive, melancholy, retiring, joining in none of the diversions,
only looking on, or languidly asking a question
now and then.   I felt what service she required
of me, and made the talk—no very difficult
matter, for the Captain and I had many acquaintance in common.   He knew some of my
own people, besides, and was able to tell me
that a young pickle of a cousin, who had taken
to the Navy, had lately joined the 'Tanis' for
service on the China station.

'The " Tanis " was here three years ago,'
said Victoria, very softly, but looking up at
the Captain, I thought, in a rather wistful
way.

'I know she was ; I boarded her at Ports-
mouth, when she went out of commission.
They all talked of nothing but your little
Island, and made me long to come here.'

'You knew the midshipman of the "Tanis,"
perhaps,' said Victoria, still with her peculiar
'inward' air.   'Where is he now?'

'What midshipman?' the Captain very
naturally asked.

If Victoria knew the name, she did not care to give it. 'He was a tall young gentleman,' she said with more animation, yet with a pause to give the Captain time to collect his thoughts after each item of the inventory; 'fair—a quick way of speaking—a pleasant laugh. If you ever heard him sing, you would be sure to remember him.' The Captain shook his head.

'He fought the battle with the slave-dhow, on the west coast of Africa.'

'What battle, my dear girl?'

'*The* battle,' she repeated.

'Do you mean he was in a boat that ran down one of those rascally traders? We do that every day.'

'He won the battle, that's all I know,' said Victoria. 'He told me so. I believe they called him " Curly " in the mess, because they were jealous of his hair,' she added, blushing to find herself forced into these particulars, but determined to have him recognised.

'Curly,' mused the Captain, doing his very best—'can't say I know the name.'

'He wore a dirk to fight with,' said Victoria.

'They all wear dirks,' returned the Captain.

'His laugh was so pleasant!' She was repeating herself beyond question, but, perhaps, it was only to give the Captain one more chance.

'No doubt, no doubt!'

'Yet some liked his smile better.'

'Some like one thing, some another,' said the Captain—feebly, I thought, but he was hard pressed.

'I suppose they all wear buttons like this?' she said, producing the uncouth ornament from her neck.

'Yes, one middy's button's like another middy's button, you know; that's the worst of it,' said the Captain; 'and it's just the same with their dirks and their heads of hair. They seem to turn all the young dogs out of one mould. I think they ought to be stamped for identification.'

Victoria withdrew into the shade of the room.

The next morning was the last morning; yet who would have guessed it? It began just as the others had begun, with early wanderings on the breezy hills, with laughter, with the giving and taking of tokens. It went on like the other mornings, only now the ship had landed the last of our simple stores, and her boat was waiting to take her people off. She was to fire a Royal Salute, as she left us, by particular request, and to hoist the Royal Standard, and man the yards. The girls seemed merrier than ever at the prospect of it. The Captain, at the head of his officers, stood at the landing-stage; the Ancient faced him, with his smiling subjects in the rear. There was but one more ceremony, and it was accomplished when the two grasped hands, as the boat, now freighted with our departing guests, with one strong shove, left the shores of the Island.

Then, for a truth, the womankind seemed to feel that it was parting, and a cry went up from them as blood-curdling as a cry of 'Murder!' heard in the night. It was the fatal gift of intensity in extremes common to these southern natures. The place of gladness was, in a moment, turned into the place of grief; they threw themselves on the ground, and bit their dishevelled hair; they stretched supplicating hands towards the boat. It

was a tropic storm of woe. Never had I
seen such utter abandonment of the very hope
of hope. It made one sick to think of the
pain there is in the world—the pain that clings
like a shadow to every joy, and that sets its
seal on every decisive fact of being, from
birth to death, on the going out, equally with
the coming in, as though to forbid all false
comfort in the belief of mere alternation. For
alternation there is not; with a wail begins
the dismal account of human experience, and
with a groan it ends, whatever may come
between. Poor wretches! bloated out of all
beauty with the water of their tears, I could
have killed them as they grovelled there, for
very rage of pity. Anything to stop these
dreary sequences of sorrow. The three days
of beatitude are past; and, for the promise
of all the coming years, listen to the Ancient
as he turns away :

> ‘Never again with thee, Robin !
> Never again by the light of the moon.’

CHAPTER XIII.

A MISSION.

A DEEP melancholy, an extreme lassitude follow our great bereavement. 'Tis as though Death had passed over us, and his lingering shadow still blighted the sunlight of the Isle. We turned to work again, but, at first, only like automaton figures. There is the action of labour, but little effect. We eat and drink in much the same mechanical way. A bird's-eye view of us would suggest something in wax-work on a grand scale. Our talk is depressing as a demonstration on the phonograph, the topics indifferent, the tones a mere resurrection of the voice. No one speaks of the ship that is dead and gone.

Victoria, whose personal share in the common sorrow can be but small, seems to grieve as much as any of us. I am not allowed to be with her now—rather I see she does not want me, and I keep away. When she starts for the Peak, I start for the Watcher's Cave, and we pine on opposite heights. Her simple household duties done, she will disappear for the whole day. I pass a good deal of time in the Ancient's library, reading yellow British classics, out of the old scuttled ship. They are interleaved with book-marks, each a delicate feminine finger beckoning to a place of refreshment and rest. It is a question of time and season, and perhaps Victoria herself will tell me when to speak.

But I tire of waiting at last, the sooner because, till now, she has shared all her thoughts with me ; and, one day, I track her to a silent shelter of woods south of the ridge. She lies in the high grass, picking a flower to pieces, but otherwise quite still.

'Victoria.'

'Ah ! thinking of you has brought you,' she says, turning her head with no surprise.

'How could I know you wanted me ? '

'I did not know it myself till to-day.'

'Why must *you* suffer, Victoria ? '

'I do not suffer at all as you think; but they do; anyone can see that.'

'Well, that is their concern, or, at most, your father's. You are not Governor of the Island.'

'I am the Governor's daughter,' she said, in another tone. 'And what can my father do? What can anyone do, but you, perhaps? You must help us. Only you *can* help us. We are a poor lost people, without you.'

'What do you mean?'

'This sorrow——'

'Will pass in a week. Let it run its course.'

'I do not want it to pass like that, to die of mere numbness. So much else will die along with it, if it does.'

'Fight it down.'

'No, no, no! What a bludgeon man you are! You must be killing something. And you can't kill a sorrow or a weakness by what you call fighting it. Perhaps it will kill you instead. I know; do you think I have never had to try? Now listen to what I say. Whenever you are weak, or whenever you are bad, you are not to go into battle with

your own heart and twang off little texts at
it. Heart will put on its casing, and turn the
points of the texts ; or, perhaps, twang back
at you, and you will both be wounded and
worried, that's all. And, if you win, you
have either a corpse before you, or a slave,
and there's a nice union till death do us
part ! '

'You are to run away, perhaps. Is that
your woman's science of war ? '

'Oh, now we have heard the mocking
bird on the Island ! ' she said, in grave rebuke.
' But that is just it ; you are to run away, but
always to higher ground. Leave your weakness and your badness alone, and try for goodness, that is all. Don't waste yourself in the
marshes ; the mountain is the best place. An
old man who had lived in India with the
priests told me that, and I gave him some
yams for it. He was cook to a whaler. Yet
you say we don't know how to trade.'

' But what has all this to do with my
healing powers ? That is what puzzles me.'

' Lead us to the higher ground,' she said,
laying her hand on my arm.

' What *do* you mean ? '

'Civilise us. Make us like England. Give us larger things to live for. Tell us what we must do. There must be something wanting, but I cannot tell what it is. It all seems so beautiful here—the shining sun, friends to love, peace, the singing, the sea, the very wind in this wood! Yet I know there must be something. That is why the Queen's ships never come again. We are like children, perhaps.'

' Keep so.'

'No, no, we want to be like you. This is babyland. Make us great and good. You know the secret: you have lived *there*.'

' What am I to do?'

'Speak to father. Father will speak to the people. He does not see it as I do, but you can open his eyes. Then we'll have a meeting, and begin to be like England at once.'

It was inviting, no doubt: to be a Moses of the Pacific, and to shape a nation! Perhaps they *are* in a bad way, if one comes to think of it. I remember that test case of the barter of the yams. It seemed nothing in passing; it is everything, if you look at it in the proper light. What poverty of spirit! they cannot

so much as dispose of a vegetable on first
principles. They have no principles at all,
only beautiful emotions; no science of life;
at best, but an unconscious art. Upon my
word, they live like so many lilies of the
field, not even like orchids, which, in a general
way, are at least brought up. They are a
mere flowery mead of humanity. By the
time I have brought them to this state, in
swift meditation, I myself might be a Scotch
landscape gardener, for my yearning to lay
them out in walks.

'Very well, Victoria; anything to make
you happy—you and yours. You wish to
have your people civilised?'

Her smile was answer enough.

'I must warn you beforehand: it hurts.'

'How else could we expect it to do us
good?'

'Sometimes you will think me your worst
enemy.'

'O! be still! when will you speak to
father?'

'To-night. But you must take care to
keep us to ourselves—us three. We want no
outsiders.'

'I will take care.'

'Now go, dear child, and leave me alone to work it out.'

She had gradually lowered her voice, as though to lull me to rest in a blessed promise and a blessed resolve. Now she ceased speaking altogether, and only looked ineffable gratitude and hope, as she stole away softly through the long grass.

CHAPTER XIV.

A PLOT.

No better opportunity could have been desired. His Excellency was very chatty that night, in mere reaction of mood, perhaps, against the prevailing gloom of the Island. We met on the lawn; and he was as full of glowing courtesies, before passing indoors to his supper, as the gracious Duncan on another occasion, while he ran the same risk of deadly intent against the peace that was his very life. I, knowing what was making ready for him, could not but feel like a Thane of Cawdor, while Victoria, I am sorry to say, filled the part of the lady of the castle. She watched me, even more than she watched him, and whenever I showed symptoms of recoil from the dreadful venture, she impelled me by a look.

'We're getting better, sir,' he said cheerily

when he had finished his meal, 'but it's a slow cure. I'm going to fine some of 'em to-morrow for cutting the trees. It'll wake 'em up, and give 'em something else to think about. Not but what things might have been worse; only three new love-knots, according to my reckoning, four initials with crown and anchor, two hearts with arrows, one ditto without—and I think I've been all over the place.'

Now for it.

'What else can you expect, my friend? They must do something. Things are rather slow here.'

It was the horrid first blow, and it quite staggered the poor old man.

'As how?' he faintly said.

I could have stopped for pity, but Victoria smiled at me from behind his chair. Then, I shut my eyes and struck on.

'Rather humdrum, you know. No spirit, no careers; one man as good as another, and not even a good deal better, as the saying goes.'

'It never troubled me,' he meekly said.

'Yet you are the Chief Magistrate!'

'Well, if we are in fault, sir, I shall be glad to hear of it. What's amiss?'

'Not very much, perhaps; only I think you want variety of formation, that's all.'

'We shall get it right, sir, I dare say, if it is to be got right. Please go on. You have travelled; you are able to speak.'

'Well, by variety of formation I mean the division of classes. Look at the beautiful gradation at home—an aristocracy for the fine art of life; a middle class for the moral qualities, which are not fine art, but only helps to it; a lower for the mere drudgery outside of both art and morals. The great mark of all progressive nations is that struggle of each man to make some other do his dirty work for him, which is commonly known as aspiration for the higher life. A few live in dignity, unhaste, affluence, and wear the fine flower of manners; but, to sustain the costly show, and help them so to live, the many give up all hope of these things on their own account, sometimes forming perfect castes, who do the dirty work from father to son, as others fill the office of Earl Marshal.'

K

'I do assure you, sir, we've nothing of that sort here.'

' This self-denying section has many names. Sometimes it is called the slave class ; but "working," or "lower" class, or "sons of toil," is usually preferred, as being the politer and less descriptive term. They engage in all the mal-odorous tasks, to the end that the others may smell sweet, and accumulate porcelain, where the conception of beautiful living is in that somewhat rudimentary stage. Now you are in a curious, not to say an un-exampled, position. You are without this indispensable class ; and how you have got on, even so far, without it is a mystery to me. Being without it, you are, of course, without the other two. Your middle term of the great combination is nowhere ; and, for your aris-tocracy, where is it to be found ? You may have your own way of bettering yourselves, but what it is I fail to see.'

' Of bettering ourselves by making others worse ? '

' Well—if you choose to put it in that way. Inequality is our religion, as a great man has so finely said. Our humblest grocer likes, in his way, to have an eldest son, and even sometimes, in modest imitation of his superiors, a youngest daughter.'

'We can't alter it,' he said, fumbling in his pocket; 'it ain't allowed under the rules.'

'A new law?' I suggested—'a sort of constitutional amendment?'

'They wouldn't stand it; that's my humble belief.'

'They might be made to stand it,' I said darkly.

'Who's to make 'em?' asked the Chief Magistrate.

'Hum!'

But his Excellency said nothing to help me out.

'You've no one you could rely upon, I suppose, if you thought it necessary to save society—no band of patriots devoted to your person—no arms?'

'There's the public hammer; that's all I know of.'

'Well, well; turn it over in your mind. See what we have done at home. A few centuries ago we were no better off than you;

every man with his bit of land for tillage, his common for grazing, a rather demoralising plenty in every hut—no really efficient slave class, in fact. But a patriotic nobility soon put a stop to that, enclosed the commons, broke up the small farms, and made a proletariat that is, to this day, the wonder and envy of the world. Then began industrial and imperial England. The old state was England for the English; but really they did not know what to do with it; the new one is, England for her betters—and see where we are now.'

'Ah! it is wonderful how you manage things over there; it's like a piece of watchmaking. But, bless you, our fingers are too clumsy.'

'You have to master the principle of the movement—that is all. Teach a whole community to unite riches with righteousness as the object of its hunger and thirst; and the thirst, especially, will beget a tremulous cerebral excitement which will keep it always on the go. Do not carry this to excess, for it will never do to have your social movement confounded with the drinker's "jumps." Only remember

that, as we argue, no wealth—no luxury;
no luxury—no crumbs for Lazarus.'

' Oh, dear!' said Victoria.

'Oh, deary, deary me!' said the Ancient,
wiping his brow.

'You yourself might set an example in this
matter. Such things often grow from very
small beginnings. The Island diet, I perceive,
is chiefly fish and vegetables. Now, in your
position as Governor, you should eat meat
at least three times a week. It would mark
a difference; and, by-and-by, you might
manage to get the more toothsome things,
such as the sweetbreads and the guavas,
reserved for your own table. The great principle is, not—as, I fear, you imagine—that one
man's best of service ought to count like
another man's best, in respect of his right to
the needful things of life, but that, on the
contrary, each bit of human helpfulness should
be weighed in a balance, and more pudding
given to those whose morsel weighs most.
The nice adjustment of the quantity of the
pudding to the nature of the service is our
economic and, indeed, our moral ideal. We
have long since given the requisite superfluity

to our governors and other men of action; now the cry is, " More pudding to the seers; " and it is one of the most exhilarating cries of the day, in its evidence of our progress in true spirituality. A great preacher, a great penman, a great revealer of the beautiful in plastic art, soon has his plate heaped up.'

' But won't the others get less ? ' said Victoria, now beginning, I thought, to repent of her part in the plot.

' O yes ; but the others are stupid.'

' They are brothers.'

' Only by courtesy, I think you will find. " Brothers in Christ Jesus," I believe, is the exact term.'

' They get hungry three times a day, all the same,' said the girl, flashing revolt.

' I am afraid you will begin to think I want to civilise you against your will,' I returned, after a pause.—The rising was quelled.

' Then, excuse the remark, my friend, but your Church puzzles me a little. I see no hierarchy, to use the proper expression ; no grade upon grade, each, as aforesaid, enjoying more pudding than the one below, until, with the highest, we reach a tableland covered with acres of this delicacy. To tell the honest truth about it, the Church began in a very small way, and it will not do to ignore the fact that the old stable has become a prosperous house of business, with a frontage in the best thoroughfares. Some of the Apostles, respectable as they undoubtedly were, must have smelt strongly of fish—though modern research has, I believe, discovered that they were not mere hands before the mast, but owners of smacks. Their successors—this Bishop from York or Canterbury, this Cardinal Prince from Rome—never offend in that way. Their lives testify to their faith in a manner that must carry conviction to the most sceptical minds. They do not merely say that religion is a good thing, and an all-sufficient, for this world and the next; they show it forth. Step into their houses—hangings and raiment of price, cabinets of medals, rarest parchments, bindings, curios, gems of painting, six courses and dessert every day but fast-day, and kickshaws innumerable to make a mere gastronomic symbol even of that. Their very pastoral staves are wrought

in fine gold ; and, to preclude all possibility
of their employment in coarser uses, are so
adroitly filled in with ornament that, by no
exercise of human ingenuity, could they be
made to hook so much as a leg of lamb. Thus
has a religion of humility been saved from its
earlier accidental association with low life, and
become a calling fit for a gentleman, until the
middle, and even the upper, classes have not
disdained it, nor professional investors of
talent considered it unworthy of their regard.
All its original difficulties as a creed of morbid
self-denial have been cleared away by the
beautiful modern development of the symbol.
Is it awkward to watch and work for the
needy, day and night? Well, wash their feet
at Easter, and you may wash your hands of
them for the rest of the year. In my travels
have I seen an Emperor and an Archbishop
condescending to this exercise, one quite busy
with the scented water, the other at hand with
the *serviette* of fine linen edged with lace.
'Tis a peppercorn rent of service and of compassionate deeds ; and for this, what generous
holdings in the good things of life, in park,
moorland, and forest, in palaces of splendour

that open to no wayfarer without an introduction, yet are often symbolled for boundless hospitality by some pretty device! The
symbol! the symbol! precious contrivance
for effecting a true *modus vivendi* between the
tastes of a gentleman and the duties of a creed.
With this to aid, my friend, your Church will
be the fitting mainstay of your social arrangements, being indeed truly of them, bone of
bone, flesh of flesh, its meanest curate fired
with the laudable ambition of getting on in
the world, and, to this end, not regardless of
snug spinsters with the talent laid by in the
napkin of the Three per Cents. But where are
you in all this? I ask, Where is even your
beginning of better things? What note have
you of a living Church, when you have not so
much as a great doctrinal contest to settle the
metaphysical reasons for goodness, before you
begin to be good?'

'That's what I was just thinking,' said the
Ancient; 'whereabouts are we?'

'Parties are the life of the Church: is
there no way of starting a question? Do you
do anything in pew rents?'

'No,' he said, 'there's my place a little

nearer the schoolmaster than the others, but that's only because I'm rather deaf.'

'Vestments? You could not put your pastor in bands? The great thing is to mark him off from the rest, and to give him his badge, as a being engaged in special communication with the Unseen. He is not to be like yourselves, a simple work-a-day creature, feeling his way to the law by the perpetual revelations of the conscience and the heart, and only getting a little beyond you in the knowledge of it, because he feels and labours more. No, he is to be a creature apart, interpreting a message from behind the Veil— a message delivered, not merely a meaning found. This solemn function must have its uniform ; so we think ; and, for some time, a quarrel over the cut of the uniform was one of the most stimulating exercises of our faith.'

'Quarrels are fines with us,' said his Excellency, 'but we might strike that out.'

'I do not see what father is to do in all this,' said Victoria.

'Then I am afraid I have failed to make my meaning clear. He might do everything ; he might become the father of his country by sowing the seeds of a governing caste. Your worst danger, at present, is the want of all distinction in externals between governors and governed. I have already suggested a slight improvement in the matter of domestic style. There are others. Your father dwells in the same sort of hut as his people—why not raise the roof of the hut? Six inches would do it. He is altogether too easy of approach. Is there no one who could act as chamberlain, usher, or go-between?'

'Reuben hasn't got much to do of evenings,' said the Ancient, in a musing tone that seemed to betoken no displeasure.

'That's it; live like yourself, and take your place; guide your people; rouse them out of this sloth of comfort and happiness; give them national ideals, great ambitions, great struggles.'

He shook his head. 'I really don't think you could get up a fight about anything here.'

'I don't mean that exactly; but why not have a foreign policy, and then it would all come in the way of nature? Have you no neighbours?'

'None.'

'There's that Island Reuben found out, father,' said Victoria.

'Why not place it under your protectorate?'

'There's nothing to protect, only some dead coral and a cave full of bones. Besides, it's a hundred and fifty miles away.'

'Oh, my good friend, your motto should be " distance no object," if you want to get on. But is there nothing nearer?'

'Well, there is another—only eighty miles off; but that's worse—dead coral without the bones.'

'You are certainly unfortunate. But I should protect these places, all the same, and leave a garrison. Never tell me! if you push on far enough, you must come to something to fight at last. Providence can hardly have meant you to be shut up in this place without an enemy in the world. Only take care, when you do come within touch of your fellow creatures, to have a weapon in your hand.'

The girl shuddered.—'More killing!'

'You've got to find your excuse for hitting 'em, even then,' he said.

'Oh, insist on protecting them, and that will do.'

'But how are you to find an excuse for that?'

'Why you seize one place to-day, to make good your hold on another that you seized yesterday; and to-morrow you seize one place more, for the same reason. It is a process known as " inevitable expansion "; and if only you follow it out logically, it leads you all round the world.'

'But where's the good ?'

'It employs your young men and your bolder spirits; it doubles the wealth and the luxury of your capitalists; it leaves even a few more crusts from their table for your poor ; and it provides a receptacle for your overflow of destitution when the crusts give out. In earlier days, when this system of main drainage on the colonial system was almost unknown, Nature had periodically to step in with a Black Death or a Plague to clear the heaps of human refuse away.'

'It seems rather a roundabout way, after all. Why not try to make 'em happy at home ?'

'Well, my friend, you cannot argue about these things, you must feel them. Civilisation is an acquired taste. Take your time, and let me know how you like the flavour, to-morrow night.'

Neither returned my parting salutation. The Ancient was lost in thought, and did not hear it: Victoria had stolen out to gossip with the stars.

CHAPTER XV.

REPENTANCE.

I FOUND her next morning seated on the Peak, and looking out to sea. She turned at my approach, as I came up the steep path from the market-place.

'That is where the fighting is to begin. then,' she said, pointing north and north-east into the infinite blue. 'We are to go there and look for something to kill—you said so. Father says you did not; I say you did. Oh, why must they always begin these things by killing something? Is there no new way?'

'Only just a little killing, Victoria; it will soon be over; and only aborigines to kill! I believe they hardly mind it at all. It would make you a people in no time; you have no idea how soon it would change the look of everything here.'

She stood up and turning landwards, cast

a wistful gaze over the settlement. 'I sup·
pose it *would* change things a good deal.'

'You really would not know the place
again.'

'And yet——'

'Come, Victoria, look on the bright side,
and don't go back on yourself. Where shall
we put your father's palace? He will want
a palace, or a castle, or something of the
sort, in time. He cannot always live with
Thomas and Richard and the other one, down
there. Suppose we put him on the other
Point, facing this. Then we will build a
little arbour here for you, and rail it off, and
you shall have it all to yourself.'

She answered never a word, but soon I
wanted no one to answer, for the excitement
of laying out this domain for the higher civilisation was enough in itself. 'We will keep
all this northern half of the Island for the
governing classes, and put the people on the
other. The views are so much prettier on
our side. If you could persuade your good
folk to give up the settlement altogether, it
would make a sweet little park for the castle ;
and the market-place, below, might easily

be rigged up as a preserve. I should put a
factory on the popular section. It would amuse
them. The chimney need never show, if you
know how to choose your site.'

'What is a factory?' asked Victoria.

'What is a factory? Well, a factory is—
a factory. Dear me, fair Islander, you are
sometimes too elementary for profitable talk!
A factory is a place where a number of people
work together to simplify the process of
appropriating their earnings to one. You
give them a little of it back, for provender,
and keep as much as you can for yourself.
What you keep back is called capital. They
make it all, of course, or some of their fore-
runners made it, every sou or cent. You get
it—that is the main point. Your share is
claimed as cost of superintendence, charge
for the loan of your brains, or, by-and-
by, as interest on your savings—a very
superior plea. But it all comes out of labour
—all, all, ALL. Labour does not mind, poor
thing, if you give it just enough to go on
with. According to the best authorities,
there must be, at least, one meal a day. The
half-meal experiment is discredited; it cuts

things too fine. This is the starting-point —just what will keep people alive. How much more they will insist on having is a matter of bargain between you and them. But only fight hard against their greediness, and it is astonishing how you can keep it down.'

'But why do you want to keep it down, and take so much for yourself?'

'For the use of your precious brains, for direction, for vigilance, for keeping your eye on 'em. Think how they would idle, else! There's a good deal of idling in this settlement. I caught two the other day—supposed to be hoeing potatoes—really pelting each other with wild flowers. It was in the great dip of green turf and shrubbery, just beyond the gorge. And now I think of it, why not put the factory there—on the slope; so that all you will have to do with your refuse is to shoot it out at the back door? It will take years to fill up the hollow, and when it is filled up, there are others just as good, to right and left. That is the way they make the valleys useful in Lancashire; I have seen it done. The people can have their little cottages on the edge; and, as the rubbish hardens, it makes a handy playground for the children, right under the mother's eye. Keep your eye on 'em all round, from the cradle to the grave—that's the essence of the system. So, there is your factory, Victoria, and now what are you going to manufacture? Tappa cloth! Turn it out cheap, and run it as a new kind of shoddy? Potatoes! Potato spirit! How did that man make his tipple—the fellow that went mad, and jumped off the steep place? Import machinery, and get the whiskey monopoly of the South Seas? Sugar! Are we quite in the right place for that? Taro! Why, of course :—" Taro, the new Vegetable Food! Testimonial from his Excellency the Governor of Pitcairn." How do you like that for a poster? Birds, beasts, and fishes— what can you do in that way? Sea birds! If we could get up something for ladies' hats, your father might be a rich man in ten years.'

'Oh, bother!' said she.

'I need hardly remind you, Victoria, that this is not the language of economical discussion.'

'Well, I cannot help it; you seem so fond
of beginning at the wrong end.'

'Excuse me, that is just what I was going
to say about your people here. It is all the
fault of their unhappy geographical situation.
Quite upside down, you know. I could show
you in an instant, if I had a map.'

'Yes, I know, but I sometimes wonder
which *is* the right side up. All your plans
seem to begin by taking something for yourself, everlasting No. 1; "take, take, take."
and so your world goes round. I wonder if it
would not go round as well to "give, give,
give." Think of others first; self is sure to get
its turn. How would that be, I wonder? I
do so wonder sometimes! Do the hardest
thing first, and get that right. I do not think
things can ever come right, unless you begin
by giving up. Don't you think it is just as
disgusting to make as much as you honestly
can, as to eat as much as you honestly can?
Why do you want to stuff so? That is what
I thought you meant yesterday. And you did
mean it; you may say what you like. Suppose you are cleverer than the others; well,
be thankful you can do something more for

them. That seems the natural way. Are
you sure you haven't got a twist? I only ask.
Why should brains be so greedy? All the
harm in the world that I ever saw or heard of
comes from greediness, gobbling. Give up,
give up, give up. Oh, only that makes men
different from pasturing brutes! Once I read
a natural history book, and the gentleman that
wrote it was trying to find out what made a
man a man. The two legs wouldn't do, you
know, because there's the chickens. Then
he tried "no tails?"—"no feathers?" Oh,
how he did try, taking off this and that, till the
thing seemed almost ready to put in the oven.
He made me laugh so. I came up here, and
thought about it, just like a riddle; and at last
I said, "give it up;" and then it came upon
me, all of a sudden—why that was the very
answer! That is why man is not the same as
the pasturing brutes : because he can give up,
because he can think of all, and himself as
only one of them. He is real man when he is
doing that, and real brute when he is doing
the other thing. That is what I thought you
were going to tell us last night—how much
more we could give up. Do show us how

they give up in England ; that's what we want
to know.'

'Victoria, don't be troublesome. I am
planning the estate.'

I turned and looked down upon the Island,
north, south, and west, in all its heavenly
beauty ; ah, what a dish to carve ! Blue sea,
patches of coral sand, silver cascades gushing
from the rocks ; glory of trees and flowers, of
clear skies, and of rainbow-tinted mists, fleck-
ing here and there the background of perfect
turquoise ; glory of the soft beauty of the
grove and settlement, of the wild beauty of
the hills, of the ordered beauty of the happy
mean in the plantations beyond, all visible,
from this height, to the farthest rocks that
stood firm for ever against the beat of
the waves. The delight of it came up to
me through every sense ; in its odours, from
the groves and gardens, the soft breeze sigh-
ing my way ; in its sounds, from the tinkle of
a tame goat's bell here and there, or from the
faint echoes of the woodman's axe, following,
in due measure of seconds, after the flash of the
sunlight on the polished steel. And, for sight
again, there was more of the exquisite human

life in tiny groups dotted all over the fields in
leisured toil, or in opalescent green shapes
in the water, off the far Point, that I knew to
be the bodies of diving girls.

Then, for the inner eye, the scene changed,
and I was once more on the steps of the
Royal Exchange, with that other sight below
me wrestling its way out of the London mist—
the Blessed of Dividend day; the dandy
clerks making for the turtle; the shabby
clerks making for the buns; the parson hurrying away to his preaching, as per bequest of
pious founder; the hungry-looking wretches
peddling the pocket combs; the flower girls
in their foul finery, mal-odorous of gin all this
way off, types of that fatallest of all divisions
of labour which puts the work in absolute
non-relation to the life of the worker; the
slouching beggar; the shunting policeman; the
demonstrating rabble with the average 7*s.* 6*d.*
to the hundred pockets, divided by a wall
only from the bullion wells of the Bank; the
nondescript thousands in black, and brown,
and russet, and all, all, as explained, from
the beggar upwards, tormented with the
secret itch of civilisation, all scratching on

the sly, and, with the scratching, throwing themselves everlastingly out of focus for my grand pictorial composition of a happy family of human kind.

And, as the grim pageant faded out again, I was once more back in the Blessed Isle— the Isle that I was laying out afresh for civilisation, to make it like the isle of my birth. I looked again, and hardly a point had changed in my short excursion to the other side of the world. The axe that was poised in the air was now buried in the tree, and the shining body of one of the girls had come to the surface, to catch the sunlight in its stead. Victoria was looking too, but with her head turned from mine; and, as we travelled in opposite directions round the circle of vision, our eyes had to meet at last.

I read in hers what she, I know, must have read in mine: 'Oh, the pity of it!'

And, with this pang, came a strange question. As that scene was the beginning of the disease that drove me so far afield for ease from torment, is not this scene the beginning of the remedy? For, what may be the meaning of that troubled vision of the Exchange steps, what but 'Each for himself,' and the Devil ever on the track of the hindmost, till there is but one left for first and last?   While, of this vision, the ever blessed interpretation is clear and true—'Each for all' in love, and truth, and mutual helpfulness, in real brotherhood and sisterhood—the core of the whole mystery, in morals, politics, religion, law and life.

CHAPTER XVI.

A DECLARATION.

'When are we to begin the alterations?' said the girl.

'Not yet, my Victoria! No, not yet! Let all things stay as they are, and let me stay with them, here by your side. Beautiful, perfect creature! Let me speak what must be spoken: I love you!'

A moment before I had no thought that these words would ever pass my lips. They were almost as much of a shock to me as to the girl. It had been my secret; or shall I say that it was almost a secret to me? Exquisite charm! In my calmer moments, I should have hated the thought of ever tearing this tender veil of mystery and reserve, behind which all that is sweetest in emotion dwells. To be able to love her as at first one loves the light, without analysis, was the most stimulating of joys ; to have it all set down in quantitative inventory of vows, and bonds, and declarations, might be quite another thing. Now, my heart was naked to her gaze, and I stood silent with a sort of shame.

She, too, was silent. She had taken her hand from mine, and clasped it in the other, behind her, just as on the day of our first meeting ; and there she stood, erect, contemplative, almost on the same spot. The feet were drawn together, the head was thrown back ; it was her characteristic attitude for emergencies. So had I seen her first, the beautiful piece of life, the divine animal, flawless in health and strength and freshness as a Venus of the Louvre, yet all touched with spiritual loveliness by the great eyes— fierce now, as I feared—and by the heaving breast.

'I cannot help it,' I said, with a sort of sullen passion. 'I felt so sure that I could keep this thing back that I set no guard over myself. Since it is out, take the truth. Whatever comes of it, we can never be the same to each other again.'

'We must be the same,' she said, with al the deep liquid softness in her voice, that was missing from her gaze. 'Oh! I knew this would come one day, I knew it would. And I did nothing to prevent it. The fault is all mine.'

'The fault?'

'I am the wretchedest woman that ever lived,' sobbed Victoria, suddenly sinking to the ground in a passion of tears, and beating it, in the wild despairing way of her sister-savages, when the boat took their sweethearts away—statue no longer, but very flesh and blood in every quivering nerve.

I did not try to raise her, I did not stir. In a few moments, when the paroxysm had passed, she raised herself, and then came, in the tenderest way, and took my hand, and looked straight into my eyes, this time, through the blessed dews that dimmed her own.

'You must know it. Some one else loves me. The word has been spoken. I am promised. Come with me—but never tell a living soul! Then, I should die.'

She led me swiftly to a small grove of wild trees, nestling in a dip of the rock, and thin and poor, for they saw neither the eastern nor the western sun. And, plunging into it, her hand still holding mine, then climbing again, after the sharp descent, she stopped before a dwarf-tree, where the Ancient would never have thought of looking for any infraction of his forest laws. A rude monogram was carved on the tree, with a date and two crosses.

'We cut them together on our last day,' said the girl, laying her finger on one of the crosses, 'and this was mine. This was cut from his coat the same day,' and she drew the wretched old navy-button from its nest in her pure bosom. 'Now you know all. I am promised; and if I forget it, how can I ever say my prayers again?'

The monogram was V.A., and the A., I suppose, was the baptismal initial of the mysterious Curly, who won the great battle with the slave-dhow, and whose laugh and smile divided the honours of admiration with mankind. Victoria's poor secret was hardly worth the telling, for, of course, I had guessed it long before. But what I had not guessed was this fidelity of daily, hourly re-membrance to the vanished hero of a vanished

ship—now, perhaps, firing her guns of joyous
salutation in some haven on the other side of
the world.

Did I hint this to the beautiful devotee?
Not I! One moment of temptation came, but
it passed; and I was spared the meanness of
tormenting her with a doubt. Since Curly
was her religion, let him be her religion still.
Here was his shrine. It was hung all about
with strange little memorials of him that looked
like aids to worship, votive offerings of bits of
ribbon on the branches of his sacred tree. A
necklace of shells, fastened in its place with
pins, formed a border in alto-relievo for the
monogram and the date. In due course, no
doubt, there would be an altar for the navy-
button and a temple for the altar—so such
things grow. I remembered what the girl
had told me of the old strain of idolatry in
her blood. Yet truth and love are so en-
trancing to the gaze that, in regarding them,
the real amateur soon loses all thought of self.
The picture in this virgin's soul was a master-
piece, not to be marred by a touch—Curly in
his orisons, ever praying with his face towards
the Isle; seas and continents between them,

yet the electric thread of sympathy only the longer on that account.

All this I fancied forth, and, as usual, in that kind of snap-shooting at truth, I could not be quite sure of my mark. With all her hope and trust in Curly, Victoria seemed full of a strange disquiet about him, not easy to explain.

'Five ships here since he left,' she said, 'and no word or token from him—not so much as one of these,' and she returned the button to her breast. 'The black people have killed him, perhaps. Every night and every morning this last month I have come here to ask for a sign of him, living or dead. You remember that night I saw the shape on the Ridge : I half fancied—that was why I was so afraid ; just because I was with you. Have I done anything wrong ? Have I done wrong ? Nobody helps me. I seem to stand all alone.'

'Victoria, if you talk like that, I must tell you that I am by your side.'

'Dear, good friend, yes, I seem to be forgetting you. Why is it so hard to do right ? Why is our choice always between pain and pain ? '

'You shall not choose, princess; I will choose for you. Be my comrade, and only that. I will ask for no more. As for me, let me be to you what I like, what is best for me. All wisdom is in loving you, and I want to be wise. If I must not speak to you, let me spend precious hours by your side, looking, learning, for your eyes light for me the dark places of the world.'

'Comrades then,' she said, smiling; and she gave me her hand.

CHAPTER XVII.

A MEDITATION.

So now, I think, I begin to see why I have been sent here—not to give lessons, but to take them. My education has been neglected, and I am coaching for a pass in the higher learning of life. I am reading with Victoria— reading in the deep eyes, without book. It is a course of social economy by a new method. The method is to look on this image of the Divine, as intently as may be without being caught in the act. I must not be caught; half of the gusty anger of the gods with adoring mortals comes of their dislike of being stared at. And, besides looking, there must be listening—listening with the heart. The ear will not do; the true message of this exquisite piece of being is only for a finer organ. Put a microphone in a cave, and it will register the beat of the earth's

breathing : with a still more delicate instru-
ment, perhaps, this girl's elemental nature, at
its stillest, will be heard to speak. As soon
as my heart was stirred, then truly she began
to be audible to me—blessed day !

And to give me delight, as well as profit,
she has not the faintest idea of her function.
Often I get the benefit of a whole morning's
lecture, requiring copious notes, while, for all
she knows of it, I have but watched her as
she manœuvred a battalion of fowls.

A grand provision of leisure for the true
work of life seems to be her chief instinctive
aim. She has the genius of indifference to
trivial things; she is never busy with aught
that does not truly count. The idleness of
hurry is unknown to her; she is always free
for essentials—a true word, a noble action,
a great thought.

But this is lover's talk. I cannot help
that; lover's talk let it be, so only she
cannot overhear.

I am a true lover in this, that the things
she says to me are as nothing to the things
she seems to say. I do not want her to say
much. I can say for her all I most want to

hear. She idealises the world for me. She is a sublime suggestion. She only starts the game; I play. Worship is in the worshipper. She brings out my highest, truest, best. A something is within me; she is its mystical correspondence in warm life. She seems to speak things to me, she seems to be things to me. Are these things true of her? What care I: they are true of me!

So, then, for me, she is a great artist in being. She lives to beauty, the sole end. She does naught only for the thing done; there is also the way of doing it. I note her placid disdain of a certain hen, that has an absurd habit of hatching by quantity, and addles half the brood. The other half, for want of due maternal care, are a species of bush-fowl that have lost their way in civilisation, and Victoria spends days over their bags of bone and feathers, to bring them into harmony with her great law. I am sure she thinks, though she might never know how to say it, that every problem of being is, in the profoundest sense, a problem of manner. *How* do you love, hate, suffer, and rejoice; nay, how do you eat and drink? There are higher proprieties, even in this art, than the management of peas with the fork. Is it after the manner of the farmyard, or after the other? I remember her little touch about the pasturing brutes. The brutes, too, renounce, but not as a fine art. It is only their ' needs must when the devil drives.' That was her meaning. They only do without; man *gives up*, because man alone is the artist, and art is choice. Living or dying, how slight as ends in themselves! but how you live, how you die! Is the piece well acted, or have you but got through your part? Who wants it, merely as a part got through? Not that greater than Theseus, for certain, before whom this dream-play is played.

That picture of the old life troubled me so, that grand composition of the Exchange steps. It would not come right. Here is one whose mere presence brings everything into its place. Let her but stand beside the easel, and I get the key at once. Now I see where it was wrong; now could I go among the rushing, blurred figures of my sitters, and ask them, for the love of God, and, still more, for the love of man, to keep still. I could say to

them, as at her bidding, ' Piano! piano! you
are perishing of over strain. You, the higher
up, why this frantic scraping for useless
currency? What can it do for you? How
much of peace comes out of it, how much
of fineness of life? What are you when
all is done—when you have sat at meat with
my Lord, and added the Hall in the country
to the mansion in town? Have you yet found
out the faintest inner meaning of one of the
pictures on your wall, of one of the books
on your shelf? You think Walter Map is
for monkish Latin, and that other's vision of
" all the wealth of this world, and the woe,
both " merely for a scholar's treat. *Mal-
heureux*! rushing away to your daily drive for
more canvases, more bindings, more horses
of swiftness, more furniture, in a word, and
more dinners of the stalled ox. The greed
makes the hurry, and the wasteful idle hurry
spoils the life. Oh, the grim set of your
jaws, the thinly veiled hardness of your
eye, even at the sacred hour of rest and re-
laxation! What are you but a huge river-
pike in black and white! More leisure,
friend, less lust of gear. Cut away the hin-

drances to living, and begin to live. Take nothing in but what you can digest to true use, which is beauty of life. What a scandal, if you were caught and opened in an unguarded hour, and half your stomach were found lined with vanities as profitless as the bits of shoe-leather and old corks so often found in the maw of your prototype—vanities of things bolted to the end of bolting, titles of park and meadow where *you* can never find a flower, visiting-lists where you can never find a friend, cards for music where you may never hear a note that breathes one of the secrets of Heaven. Your bolting for waste takes so much out of the common stock for use. Your grab for superfluity baulks so much honest craving for need!'

You work for it! Will no one deliver us from the tyranny of that cry? Work for what?—to have and to hold, to leave less and less for the weaker, till finally, in the lowest hell of it, the huge crowd of the uncanny have to learn to call their base scramble for your leavings the battle of life? More leisure for these, from the obsession of the one degrading thought—how to get the dry crust and the cold potato for the day's meal. For, true living begins only when such things are done with, when the belly is timbered with victual, and the back clothed, and when the spirit, that is the all-in-all, is left free for its shaping work. More leisure for love and friendship, and kindly deeds, and joy—the true business, which, if we were not blinded, would have their banks and their depôts, and their pushing agents in every street. The real ' Theory of Exchanges,' what is it but the philosophy of the diffusion of the humane self? Oh, the hard world of the self-helpers, with their Smiling apostle! oh, the hard world!—the hard world of all the workers, high and low, leisureless for profitable toil, the real task hardly so much as begun—too hard even for the very martyrs, robbed of their right to smile in the death-hour, by the horrid fear that all eternity will never set the muddle straight! Jesus, what a sight! the sight of the factories, right through, from the tiniest monkey-faced minder, up to the gaudy boss-bird in his mahogany cage. This organised labour? fie! oh fie! Organised? for what? for the sake of the labour, or for the sake of the labourer—the only product that really counts—for the sake of the cottons, or for the sake of the garment-stuff for the souls of men? Is labour man's end, or his means? his master, or his ministrant? Surely the first true end of making cottons well is to make the maker better. And, if one must be spoiled in the process, for Heaven's sake let it be the cottons, though, of that, no need. Every thread of their fineness must come out of some inner fineness in him. How pathetically absurd to have them smooth, and white, and close-textured, and firm in the pull, and him coarse, foul, loose-minded, tearing in the Devil's hand under any strain of lust or rage! But why insist on a commonplace when all the wisest feel that truth, and speak it now? The work exists for the worker; let us never cease to proclaim it, and have done with the old lie—the worker for the work. How sad the sight when you pass from one to the other! The expectation born naturally of the fine thing is always of some finer animate thing behind. Hence the craving for sight and knowledge of heroes. But see the slop-made piece of human handiwork that skulks as maker, behind the screen of drawing-room intrigue, or behind my lady's fan—shabby, shambling, beer-bedewed, only so much of him washed as might soil the satins and brocades he shapes for others' uses! Go into the dismal slums that manufacture for Mayfair, and follow the dainty casket for jewels from one end to the other of the line—from the rickety workshop, airless, and only not lightless, too, because the light is wanted for the labour, to the still daintier casket for men and women, in which it finds its cushioned rest. If this beautiful correspondence, why that grotesque incongruity? If these who touch it as owners are as fine as itself, why not, also, they who touch it as makers, at least with the inner fineness, and a certain amplitude of material life? But no: a dozen have died to all the true ends of being to make that pretty toy, have been reared in the belief that all the fineness they have is to go into that direct, and not, in the first place, into their own lives.

For nothing sanctifies a wrong, not even a headache in doing it; and 'honest industry,' which makes of patience and thrift but the foothold for its spring upon the back of stupidity or improvidence, is the sinfullest sin of all. Be not so sanctified of air, O new hot-gospeller of work! Your sole right over knaves and fools is but the right to help them to better wisdom out of your heart and hand. Your virtue was not given to you for investment at forty per cent. The knaves and fools are diseased—that is all; and you, when you stoop to personal profit out of their infirmity, are worse diseased than they. A terrible malady, yours, of hard work to self-regarding ends; infectious to the last degree; a sort of dry rot of life.

Believe this—individualism, self-help, to any other end than the help of all, is the great untruth. Believe it, in spite of the Smiling apostle, who has done more harm with the nostrum of his title than Abernethy with his invention of blue-pill. Go on being self-helpful, if you must, for thirty, forty centuries more; only not for ever! Take a lease of five times nine hundred and ninety-nine years, yet fix some term! Give us a little hope, and name the happy day when the freehold of light and life and jouissance shall revert to all.

Try the other thing as a regimen, once in a way, as a new diet for your soul's health—as a new quack medicine, then, powerfully recommended by a sufferer : will that appeal? One poor little pill—it cannot hurt overmuch. Cut off some of the work that ministers but to your ease and luxury, and that, with interest piled on interest of infamous wrong, makes the ever-growing load of sorrow for the mass. Cease to be competitive and self-helping, at least in precious moments when you feel your heart sick. Go back to it, if you will, if you can, when you feel a man again, as convalescents resume their mulligatawny and hot lobster when the plainer roast and boiled have set them right. Treat your mind like a stomach, and give it a touch of nature once in a while. Then, if you have a taste that way, still return for your gorge at the banquet of work. Only, try to include in it some concern for the most truly helpless, the stupid and the base, and to find the relish in the end rather than the means. For the end is not to make riches of mind, body, or estate for yourself, but to lift up life for one and for all.

This is how I interpret Victoria. This is what I think she means. Let me put it to the proof.

CHAPTER XVIII.

A LORD OF INDIA.

I HAVE to tell her one day of the Empire, the power, the stretch of it, the count in millions of miles, in millions of souls; the largest empires, living or dead, mostly but parishes beside hers and mine. In mere size, Russia, even, beaten by an eighth, the Grand Republic beaten all but three times over, the late Darius the Great beaten five times clear — more than forty Germanys, more than fifty Spains! Our own Mother Island but a dot in a waste beside it, Victoria's Island but a dot on the dot, the parasite of a midge. With this, the figures for commerce, the figures for sails on all the seas that wash the ball, the figures for wealth—a round nine thousand millions sterling, if we were sold up to-morrow, and, for all the bad years since 'seventy-five, a steady hundred and eighty millions added year by year to the hoard—our swelling liver almost putrid with the gorge of gold.

Victoria is delighted; wants to measure Pitcairn with her sash—is stopped; becomes light of heart, effusive; carolleth; offers to take me to the Cave on the ledge, for a treat—the Cave of the Great Scrape, I have always called it—pays me a sort of reverence, as one who has come from the sun of this colossal system—is stopped again. Then, after purring foolishly over the totals, like a great happy kitten that has got all the thread in the world for a ball, asks to have them unravelled in measured inventory. Is told something about Australia, about Canada, about the Indies. Seems to see it all with ever-dilating pupils, as a child before a pageant of pantomime. Sees it in procession of countless tribes, armies, emblemed industries, brother peoples, subject kings; warriors coated in mail, in crimson, or only in the black of their own skins; priests bearing every symbol, from the notched stick to the cross; mechanics, from them that smooth with the flint hatchet to them that smooth with the

Whitworth plane; Nature's experiments with the type, from the bushman to the man from Mayfair. At this, and long before the procession closes, shows signs of worshipping me again, as a sort of deputy lord of India and the other dependencies in Europe, Asia, Africa, and America. But I turn away.

For modesty forbids, not to speak of the fear of detection. All the lords of India are not so plump; and I sometimes wonder what the lordship means. I am a lord of India, it is true, but so is Snip there, in his sweating-shop, and Swart carrying the sandwich-board, 'lords of human kind,' as it was once put; but let us keep within bounds. I think of the lordship whenever I meet Swart, whenever I take stock of all the figures that make the huge stain of shabbiness upon our moving crowds. A lord of India, too, the man in threadbare who turns out every morning from Kentish Town or Somers, or other of the circumjacent wastes, to look for a job in the City, plodding steadily forward for the hundredth time, with fifteen shillings a week as the goal of hope. Clean shaven this lord, got up for 'respectable appearance,' down to his last ha'penny, in shining boots, inked for the cracks and patches, and shining coat; everything shining about him, but the hard and hopeless face. He is certainly of the Imperial breed—no one can deny him that—a lord of India, an heir to the ages of struggle and victory on battle plains dotting our fifth of the globe.

But Swart is the best example, and Victoria is easily stimulated to the entreaty that I will tell of him all I know. It is worth telling, in good faith.

'I first met Swart in Regent Street, a little while before I came out here. He was sandwiched between two boards of "India in London," and there was something so spiritually picturesque in the ruin of him, from his baggy hat to his mere suggestion of a boot, that it drew me to his side. I was drawn by curiosity rather than by pity, as a naturalist who might want to see how the wood-louse lives.'

'Where is Regent Street? and what is a sandwich-man?' said Victoria as I began the tale.

'We must reserve all that for the footnotes. If I am to keep on moving, you must let me get under way.'

'Well, we struck up acquaintance, Swart and I. Did I say that he was tallish, thin, bent, and grizzled, and foul? I want to get all that over as soon as may be. Sixty, or thereabouts, I should say, as to age; a not unkindly face, and not unhandsome, but for its furrows and puckers of mean cares—a good face spoiled.'

'I wish I knew what a sandwich-man is,' she murmured; 'but it does not signify. Please go on.'

'We struck up acquaintance, and I used to walk with him up and down his beat—he in the gutter, I on the kerb. He had been a soldier, and had helped to win India back for England at the storming of Lucknow. He was quite proud of the whole achievement, and of his share in it. "They was nigh slipping clean away, sir," he would say of his Indian fellow-subjects. "You cannot think how nigh they was; but we just cotched 'em by the tail." It was pleasant to see Swart proud of anything; it did so much to improve his air. At such moments, he seemed almost a man. They were but sun-rifts in a black sky, of course. Sometimes the policeman would threaten to run him in, for trespassing on the kerb with the edge of his board. This would tend to drive him wide of the gutter; then, his foreman would come by, and growl an oath at him for not walking straight in his furrow, and threaten him with the sack.'

' "The sack!" ' said Victoria softly; ' "run him in!" I am not interrupting, you know, I am only saving up.'

' I asked Swart to let me go and see him, but he said "Not yet." He was living in a common lodging-house, and he was not allowed to receive visitors. "If I was allowed," he said frankly, " I shouldn't like you to come. They really ain't fit company for a gentleman, or, for that matter, for a common man. We had three took out of their beds last night for robberies from the person, and one for burglary and murder. What with the police coming in and out of the room, and flashing their lights on your faces, there was no getting a wink. There was sixty sleepin' in our room, and the row woke most of us up. You may fancy what it was after that. Besides, I'm gettin' too old to fight for my place by the kitchen fire, and I'm cold half the time. Then, if you ain't got your fourpence every night, out you go; and I can't tackle the Embankment no more. I want a place of my own."'

'You might tell me about the Embankment now,' she said, 'but, of course, we'll make a note of it, if you are going to get cross.'

'It is an open thoroughfare, the finest in London, bordered, on one side, by gardens and public palaces, on the other, by the river. The people who cannot afford to sleep as Swart sleeps are allowed to sleep there, as a favour, for it is against the law.'

'But do you mean to say——?'

'Yes, indeed, I do; that is just what I do mean.'

'But how *can* the others go to bed, then?'

'Well, how can you, for that matter, now you know it? You get used to such things.'

'I would never go to bed if I lived there. Never, at least, till——'

'A week or two later Swart told me that his place was ready, and that I might call. He had been saving slowly for his furnishing, for, as he observed, what can you do on 1*s.* 3*d.* a day? He merely " had his eye " on a table. I let him keep his eye on it. The experiment was too interesting to be spoiled by help from me.

'His place was in White Horse Yard. White Horse Yard, you must know, Victoria. is a London slum, one of hundreds as clearly marked on the map, and as well known, as Buckingham Palace or Grosvenor Square. The description would interest you, as a semi-savage, but to us worn children of civilisation it is too trite for pleasure or profit. Every social reformer begins by describing White Horse Yard: it is the sign of the " 'prentice hand." Swart's place was reached by a narrow causeway, reeking with every kind of abomination, and by a staircase, dark and rotten, and swarming with vermin, as I had afterwards good reason to know. Here, at the summit, was his back garret, with his bed of shavings, and his table, made of a packing-case turned upside down. His neighbours worked at many trades, including that most ancient one of private plunder. The front garret was the home, as distinct from

the place of business, of " one of them gals."
Swart could never be induced to be more explicit. On the floor below, they made lawn-
tennis aprons at threepence a dozen, and
army coats. They did something with rabbit-
skins in the back drawing-room, for, one day,
when Swart opened his window for air, we
were nearly choked with a furry adulteration
of the precious fluid that came in with the
fog. A housebreaker who had been out of
work for six months or more, owing to an
injury received in a scuffle with a policeman,
occupied the front kitchen, and, by general
consent, he was the quietest man in the house.
The back kitchen—but no, nothing of these
premises below the ground level, if you please ;
nothing, even in distant allusion, in veiled hint ;
nothing about the back yard either, or about
the water-butt therein ! If you are going to
be foolish, Victoria, I shall just leave off.'

'I am not foolish.'

'What are you crying about ? '

'If we let people live so, we should be
afraid of God ; I think we should be afraid
of every thunderstorm.'

'The lightning is very tender with us

—a chimney-stack now and then ; seldom the steeple of a church.'

'It is not true. You are just saying things to me. There are missions in all the cities to look after the poor people. I have read books.'

'Of course. There were four missions in this very circumscription of Swart's, and one Inspector of Public Health.

'The chief thing the missionaries preached was the sanctity of submission, or that sanctity of property which had made this dismal hole what it was. They preached it in a pair of parlours, only less dismal than Swart's garret. Their object was to effect a change of heart as a condition precedent to the change of linen—the cart before the horse. Of the night of material ugliness around that was, on one side, the parent of all this spiritual ugliness, they seemed to have no idea. On Sunday, some of the poor people in the yard went to the preaching, dubiously, yet still hoping there might be something in it, their dim intuitions of logic being hardly strong enough to expose the mockery of its gospel of love. Others went to the drink-shops, and they were the wiser, for they found a little brightness there. There was one drink-shop to every two hundred inhabitants; and the missionaries, who were quite as dull as their hearers, never understood the reason why.

'Swart read his paper meanwhile, and joined the crowd in the "pub," when he had a penny to spare. He never missed his paper, being quite a hopeful kind of fool, and inclined to believe that the better luck was just going to begin. He had revelled in that anticipation, from Sunday to Sunday, for at least five-and-thirty years. The foreign intelligence, especially, used to cheer his soul. We were always taking something to round our Empire off; soon it would be quite trim, and then! "You may reckon we've got Burmah, sir," he said to me one day, when news came of the execution of a fresh batch of dacoits. "It's as good as ours. There'll be fine times, I'm thinking, soon. Such a rumpus, indeed, when it's all for their good!" He was really angry with the Burmese. He regarded their war, and all the other little wars, as only so many accidents of human perversity that tended to defer the grand opening of a vast humanitarian entertainment known as "Better times all round." He had hoped the curtain was going to rise, when India was quieted down, in the pit. Then came the stupid interruptions from the Abyssinian and Ashantee sections of the gallery. Then the Afghan and Zulu fights at the doors. Next, "them there fellers in the Soudan." Now, "the Burmah lot." Swart had been waiting through all this for a curtain that never stirred.'

'The curtain is to hide the stage when they are changing the scenery,' she said, wandering from the subject for a moment, like the big child she was. 'It is let down five times in most of Mr. Shakespeare's plays. I know.'

'Yes, you know, Vickey, and so did Swart. Swart was just the man for that kind of stage-play, being one of those profounder fools who take everything as it is offered to them, and who will very contentedly accept two deal boards and a sheet of canvas for a blossoming tree. They had told him that he, too, was a lord of India, and he believed it; and he was quite touched, as with the sense of an accession of personal dignity, when his Sovereign was made Empress as well as Queen. As he would often observe, all the people in his court were lords of India, if they only knew it, heirs to the Great Mogul—for he had a smattering of history—conquerors at Plassey, Mooltan, Moodkee, Sobraon, and the rest. All Clare Market and Collier's Rents, and all the Minories had their share in that great heritage, yet they never gave it a thought.

'They could not be got to see it in that way, there was the difficulty. Swart had endless arguments with them on the calm Sabbath afternoons, while they waited at the street corners, ankle deep in slush, for the opening of the houses. He would hurl his figures at their heads; totals for imports and exports, the growth in shipping, the growth in trade. There was sometimes an inert obstructive force in their stupidity against which he could not prevail. The brighter witted mocked him openly, and always led the argument back from the pageant of Empire to his own rags. The duller merely spat, but there was dissent in their expectoration ; and sometimes he was obliged to fancy they spat at him. He would ask me for help in his ˌstrait, and I lent him some of the popular literature of Federation, where the right arguments are all set down.'

'We have begun praying for Federation, every Sunday—just after the Collect. The schoolmaster is writing a Federation hymn.'

'Try to interrupt me as little as you can, my dear. It checks the flow. Make notes, and we'll settle it up afterwards.' (She took off her girdle and tied a knot for ' Federation.')

'But I felt less interest in Swart's dealings with others than in his dealings with himself. That was the ever-present wonder. I found, on probing his wound of penury, that he had been waiting for relief, not for five-and-thirty years merely, but, in a sense, for five hundred. He was of a most ancient stock, as indeed are most of us, if you will but think of it ; and for all the years it had flourished on this earth, in so far as the straining vision could trace it through the night of time, that stock had never escaped from its parent dunghill. And Swart's gaze carried back very far. For a man of his class, he had a quite exceptional knowledge of family history, partly oral, partly recorded on the fly-leaf of a family Bible, which, for the purpose of our researches, I lent him the money to get out of pawn.' (She tied another knot at ' pawn.')

' The Swarts knew themselves as far back as Anne; nay, with allowances and conjectural emendations, as far back as the second Charles. Here, then, was my opportunity, unique, as far as I know, to get at a real pedigree of a Poor Stupid ; how infinitely more interesting than any pedigree of the baronage, if only by reason of its rarity. I encouraged him, therefore, by every means in my power, to leave the current affairs of the Empire for a season, and to talk about the past of his own race. He was nothing loath, and, after weeks of labour, we had a family tree drawn out for him that, for hoary age, might not have been unworthy of a seventh Earl. We had sometimes to make a perilous leap from bough to bough, as in the best performances of this description, but we kept that secret to ourselves.'

CHAPTER XIX.

PEDIGREE OF A POOR STUPID.

' Swart then, to cast it in proper form, was of
the Swarts of Norfolk, and his family had
been settled in that part of the country from
an extremely early time. They had subse
quently removed to London, and had planted
offshoots in many of the great towns, but their
earliest family seat was a swineherd's hovel
on the bank of one of the Broads. Swart's
father, Jeremiah Swart, more commonly
known as " Jerry," had assisted at the rise of
our great cotton industry, not exactly as one
of the cotton lords, but as one of the others.
Swart had often heard his history from his
own lips. He was born in 1800, and in 1816
he took another infant to wife, without the
formality of a visit to the parson. Babes of
every age, from five and six upwards, were
common enough in the factories at that time,

and they worked from twelve to fourteen and fifteen hours a day. Puberty began early, for the temperature of the factories was the temperature of Bombay, yet, even with this chance in their favour, half the children never reached a marriageable age. They perished like flies, and the few that were left, like flies of a certain sort, had just time to arrange for the propagation of their species, and then to die. Boys and girls, men and women, worked together, lived together. Inspection was unknown; control of any sort, on the part of law, equally so; their common lodging-houses, not to put too fine a point on it, were common stews. They toiled for just as much as would keep their bodies together; and the rate of pay was calculated on the sound economical assumption that they had no souls.

'Swart's father seems to have taken the same interest in public affairs as his more famous son. He would often tell the boy of his patriotic satisfaction in the Act of 1816, which regulated the detention of Napoleon at St. Helena. He felt, as he used to say, that they had got Boney safe at last, and he could now breathe as freely as his fluffy cough would allow. Swart's infant mother was indifferent to that great event, for she was bearing Swart in her bosom, at the factory, within three days of her delivery of him into this joyous world. Having performed this function, she went to join her ancestors, whose pedigree, I regret to say, it is impossible to trace. Swart's father used to remark that he had been less fortunate than Prince Leopold, who, on taking the Princess Charlotte to wife, at about this time, secured 50,000*l.* a year with her, dead or alive. He meant to say, of course, that the grant was to be continued to the Prince in the event of the lady's demise. It was a generous gift, for the nation had been left in extreme poverty and misery by the great war. The Marquis Camden subsequently surrendered his sinecure, " towards the relief of the public burdens," in the handsomest way in the world, and the Prince Regent found he could spare 50,000*l.* a year from his own ample revenues, for the same purpose. Swart's father was particularly touched by this last act of self-denial, and he expressed a hope that his Prince might never want a meal. The wish must have been heard in

Heaven. The people at large were not so fortunate: they became like wild beasts with hunger; they rioted at Ely, they rioted at Spa-Fields. The country blazed with incendiary fires, as though for a second celebration of the Peace. The hero who had conquered the Peace was not forgotten; and Strathfieldsaye was purchased for the Duke of Wellington.

'Swart's father had once enjoyed the felicity of seeing his Grace, and had taken so careful a note of him that he knew the number of buttons on his blue frock-coat. It was not his only souvenir of greatness :— " Father once met the Marquis of Waterford, when his lordship was out on one of his larks. The Marquis gave father a black eye, and half a crown."'

Victoria knotted something again : I fancy it was ' black eye.'

' Darkness covers the Swarts for a brief space, but in the middle of the eighteenth century they flash into view again with " Father's great grandfather," sold into the Plantations for indigence, in the flower of his age. Some of the workers had their fixed term of servitude, just like the burglars now ;

their masters were at liberty to whip them, and to impose additional years of servitude, if they ran away. "He got nabbed in a rumpus," says Swart, "when they was taking old Commodore Anson's treasure to the Tower. You look in the books, sir; you'll find that right. This here Commodore had sailed round the world, and had made many rich prizes; and a million and a quarter in treasure was taken down to the Tower to be stowed away. There was thirty-two waggon loads of it, the old man counted 'em, and somehow our family's never forgot the number. All our sort turned out, as you may fancy, to see the waggons go by. Father's grandfather was a bit pushed at the time, and used to sleep on a brick-kiln, with a few other chaps out of luck. There was no sleep that night; they couldn't have closed their eyes, he said, if it had been a bed of down. It was such a great day for England! They all sat up singin' songs out in the fields, till it was time to start and see the procession. The old man allus said he wasn't a bit drunk, for he hadn't tasted bite or sup that day. It was the sight of the waggons, somehow, seemed to make him turn faint. Anyhow, I suppose he behaved foolish, for they collared him, and as I told you, he was sold off. He couldn't give no account of hisself—they've allus been very hard on you for that. Father's grandfather's wife went out after him, all the way to this 'ere Plantation, wherever it was. It took her three months to go, but she lost his address, and so she had to come back. They never met again. She once did some washing for Mr. Pitt, him that was made a nobleman : you'll find that right. She died at the washtub, that was the end of her. She was a game 'un, she was ; no mistake about that ! " '

Poor Vickey ! I see the great drops gathering, and I know they are just going to roll over : so I push on.

' " Some of our women didn't turn out so well. I don't want to foul my own nest, sir, you understand, but it's sometimes a great struggle in a poor man's family to get enough to eat for growing gals. They always aimed above 'em though, our women did : I will say that. One of 'em took up with a master bootmaker in Bond Street by the name of Simmons—made for the Royal Family. That

was my grandmother, as she might be called.
I've heard that I might give myself the name
of Fitz-Simmons, if I chose, but Swart 'll do
for me. I only mention it to show that she
had not demeaned herself so much as some
might think.

'" Father's grandfather was the man in the
corner of one of Mr. Hogarth's pictures—the
one 'avin' his 'ed battered with the pewter.
Ah, they was 'igh old times!"

'I could but regard this reference to a
family portrait as another note of antiquity of
race. There was even some trace of a family
library in a street ballad sung by a progenitor
of Swart at the Coronation of George IV., and
still in excellent preservation between the fly
leaves of the book of Truth. In rugged, but
heartfelt and effusive verse, it called on the
whole earth to rejoice. A family museum of
curios, often another note of lineage, was
wanting, except in so far as it might be found
in a red waistcoat that had belonged to Mr.
Townsend, the famous Bow Street runner, who
had "once locked grandfather up." Swart
had heard that it was worth money, but he
could never get more than sixpence on it at

the tally shop, and he had offered it in vain to Madame Tussaud.

‘ Here the Bible record, and Swart's memory of the direct oral tradition ended, but I could not have his story stop. I, therefore, went down to the Heralds’ College, and to the Record Office, and by liberal fees to certain yellow men called searchers, found out a good deal more. They proved to me beyond question, as I had long expected, that the Swarts had been always with us as actors in the great drama of history, only the managers had not thought it worth while to give them a line in the bills. As soon as I made it worth while to search beyond the bills, Swarts seemed to become as plentiful as blackberries. We found that nothing had been done without them. Dig down into the foundation of any fair structure of Imperial greatness, and you were pretty sure to come upon a Swart, if only as rubbish for the filling-in. One of them was certainly among the two-and-seventy thousand vagrants hanged, or otherwise despatched, in the reign of Bluff King Hal. They were enclosing a good deal at that time, and the Bluff one had broken up the monasteries, where the Swarts had often found a meal. These operations filled the country with vagrants, and the vagrants had to be removed. They were flogged, and fined in one of their ears, for a first offence, and hung up like flitches, for a second, and thus effectually cured. A Swort or Swyrt, of Norfolk, which, as before stated, was their country seat, had been branded as an able bodied loiterer as far back as 1547.

'To form an idea of their situation, one must watch a fly trying to crawl out of a pot of jam. You leave him there in the morning : you find him there at night. Never, never, in the summer's day, nor in dateless eternity, shall that fly get clear!'

'You talk cruel on purpose : somebody just helps him out.'

'Victoria, give me a chance! Suppose nobody helps him. When, by heroic labour, he has cleared his forelegs, his wings are still coated with the sugary mire ; and, as he plants the forelegs down, to attend to the rest of him, the forelegs are besmeared again. Let him resolve to leave them behind, in his desperation, and he will but lose his balance,

and foul the wings once more. Poor fly!
Poor Swart! Poor, Poor Stupids! whose
history through the ages is my humble theme.
The only difference is that the Swarts are
sunk in slime instead of jam, and that they
have the power of breeding there, and leaving
their heritage of fruitless struggle to countless
generations. Always the slime is peopled
with this race, and never shall they get out,
till God send a brother to scrape them. The
tragi-comedy of the situation is found when
one, by miracle of discovery of a brother's
body for foothold, wriggles himself free, and
then stands on the brink, to comfort the
others with Penny Readings from the author
of " Self Help."

'For full seven centuries, as I could trace
it now, had the Swarts been waiting for the
deliverer with a potsherd. Their history was
a history of illusions in the belief that he had
come at last. Once, clearly, they thought it
was Kett, for there was a Swart in his re-
bellion in 1549. I hear him at their foolish
Litany of human rights: "Look at them
and look at us! have we not all the same
form, are we not all born in the same way?'

Eternal protest! Nature's everlasting whisper
to the innermost heart of man—never sufficiently answered by a knock on his head
from the outside! The Earl of Warwick and
his mercenaries were prompt enough with
this response, yet the Swarts were still un-
convinced. There was a Swyrte—I can but
think it was the same family, and I am
confirmed in that opinion by one of our
kings-at-arms—in Wat Tyler's affair, in the
fourteenth century. The conjecture is that
he was one of the "landless men," whom the
lawyers of the time were trying to bring back
into serfage, after their extremely informal
manumission by the Black Death. Nearly
sixty thousand persons, it may be remembered, perished of that pest in Norwich alone,
and this had probably convinced the Swyrtes
that it was time to be stirring. A sort of
insane joy in the ravage wrought by the dis-
order, as in a clearance for right and freedom, by the Devil as redeemer, is apparent in
some of the sayings of the time; and the
surviving Swyrte in the train of Tyler may
have felt, in his extremity, that he was open
to a fair offer from that other side. The

sentiment is perhaps hereditary, for I remember to have noticed a strange elation in the Swart of the Victorian era, when the late visitation of Asiatic cholera was threatened, or as, I fear, he took it, promised, to our shores. His manner exhibited the tremulousness of a great uncertain hope, and his reading of the telegrams from Marseilles and Paris in his Sunday paper took a rhythmic cadence. as though they were portions of a saga. The circumstance is perhaps, incidentally, suggestive of his Norse descent, but we must not go too far. Local Kentish records tend to show that the earlier Swyrte just mentioned had risen to a certain eminence in the movement, the highest perhaps the family ever attained, for a man of that name undoubtedly acted on one occasion, as deputy tub-bearer to the " mad priest of Kent," John Ball. Ball. as we know, was preaching, five centuries ago, just what they are preaching at Clerkenwell Green to-day. " Good people, things will never go well in England so long as goods be not in common, and so long as there be villains and gentlemen. But what right are they whom we call lords greater folk than we?

Why do they hold us in serfage? If we all came of the same father and mother, of Adam and Eve, how can they say or prove that they are better than we, if it be not that they make us gain for them by our toil what they spend in their pride? They are clothed in velvet, and warm in their furs and their ermines, while we are covered with rags. They have wine and spices and fair bread; and we eat oat cake and straw, and water to drink. They have leisure and fine houses; we have pain and labour, the rain and the wind in the fields. And yet it is of us, and of our toil, that these men hold their state." We may easily imagine the effect of such words on one of this stupid race.

'When Ball was thrown into prison, his deputy tub-bearer seems to have joined Tyler as a man of action, for the name turns up in a rude muster-roll of the gathering at Blackheath. He was possibly one of the band that forced their way into the Tower, and pulled the beards of the scandalised knights, promising to be their equals and good comrades in the time to come. He never came within touch of chivalry again, unless he happened

to be among that village remnant of revolt
that fell under its maces in the wood at
Billericay, after a two days' fight, for " the
same liberties as their lords."   But this is only
matter of supposition, and it is more likely
that the Swyrte of Blackheath simply sneaked
into town on the death of his leader, to root
his offshoot of this great family in the London
slime.

'I cannot find any trace of a Swart at
Cressy or at Poitiers, though many of that
sort unquestionably left their bones in France.
They were not without a monument, however,
but it was in their works. *Circumspice.* It
was in the wasted fields of Aquitaine, the
stretches of utter solitude, the patches of
direst poverty, league upon league of burnt
homesteads, and of famine-struck hordes going
mad with misery and rage. For the French
lords being captive, the French serfs had
naturally to raise the money for their ransom,
and the agony of the operation at such a
season of ravage drove them into sheer revolt.
The captive lords, after the manner of their
order, exhibited an admirable self-control;
and, with much dignity, took their meals with

the family in the English castles, while they awaited the remittances that were to set them free. So blood will always tell! The Swarts of England, to their ruin, had wrought this ruin to the Swarts of France—as it was in the beginning, and, probably, ever shall be, world without end. Victoria, there is a final word!'

But she only smiled faintly, and shook her head.

'Here, I confess, I quite lose the scent of this interesting race, strong as it must naturally be. That some of them were doing something at the time of the Conqueror, the heralds, and even the physiologists, assure me is beyond a doubt. I have looked for them in the Bayeux Tapestry; and in one prostrate figure that is being used as a foot warmer, while his betters are presumably enjoying a view of the English landscape, I fancy I recognise the family nose. For my own part, I am tolerably certain that some of them were alive at Troy time, and that somebody was sitting on them then.

'A wonderful old family, the Swarts, the Percys of the record but a set of *parvenus* beside them, a family that, in all ages, has

helped to make the dark background for the
picture of the beauty and the pride of life ;
for the frolic group of Chaucer, for Cressy's
firework blaze of triumph, for the Armada,
for Blenheim, and for Waterloo ; for the
grandiose spectacle of pomp and vanity in
every field.   Hey! for the idle literature that
all this while could sing its blasphemous song
of perfumed bowers, while the wynd reeked ;
for the idle art that could find nothing more
serious than a scheme of colour in the con-
trast between these Royal purples and these
beggar's browns!   And hey! for the old, old
Swarts, the true Ancients of Days!   Surely
they are as venerable as the Vedas, and, beside them, the best of merely historic stocks
is but a mushroom growth.   What a struggle
among the tuft-hunters to get the Swarts to
dinner, could they but see this!   Such a
family only want a blazon, to commend them
to the world.   I would suggest a Jackass,
gules, between a stick (uplifted) and a bundle
of wet hay.   Motto (the same as that of the
old King of Bohemia—blind, like the whole
race that bear it in good faith): "I serve."
Crest : a Fool's cap.   Ever has that cap of

the Swarts gone up for the victory, while the caps of the Swarts' leaders have been held out for the reward. How have the Swarts shouted, honest folk, as province after province rolled into the mass of Empire, till it stretched beyond the purview of the sun !

'Whatever he had lost through the ages, Swart's joint-stock lordship of India remained, and he was proud of it, as I have tried to show. A Lascar was associated with him, as a boardman, in the Indian exhibition : they were the best of friends, but Swart made a point of walking first. It was a question of mere precedence, and it was not unkindly done ; they always took their pipe together, at the midday halt in the mews. The Lascar was really Swart's hierarchical superior, in a business point of view. He received three-pence a day more than the others, because his complexion was suited to the character of the show. With this natural advantage, and with a turban manufactured with rare self-denial from the tail of his own shirt, he was altogether a specialist of publicity for such things as Indian Bitters, and the Turkish Bath. He was more of a philosopher than

Swart. He had accepted caste as a law of Nature and of God, while the other, in the muddled English way, only took it as it came. He could give chapter and verse for it from his holy books. "For the sake of preserving the Universe, the Being supremely glorious allotted separate duties to those who sprang respectively from his mouth, his arm, his thigh, and his foot"— Read the Dharma Sāstra; and be still!

'But the difference, as he was wont to observe, did not end here, for the foot is a thing of five toes, and there are toes, and toes. Chancing one day to meet in the gutter another Lascar, whom he suspected of a descent from the little toe, he spat on the ground, and exhibited every sign of repulsion, though his countryman, who was advertising an Arabian gum-drop, was in the same business as himself, and, to all appearance, was as good a man. There were really three toes between them, as he explained to Swart.

'There had been an attempt to bring him into the fold of Christianity, but it broke down. He had been led to the gate by a member of a special mission who, without his knowing it, had given his colleague of the little toe a rendezvous at the same place. He endured the hateful presence as best he might, until the rite of Communion required him to touch the cup that had just been pressed by the other's lips. Then he set down the un-tasted pledge of love and brotherhood, and turned away.

' He had brought his lady over with him, and she lived in the seclusion of a White-chapel zenana, in continual fear of the effect of our foggy climate on her lord's remaining lung. She was far from her own people, and if she became a widow, how could she hope to be treated with the requisite indignity during the funeral rite? Burning was, of course, out of the question, but who would tear out her nose-ring, and the cartilage with it, in the regular respectable way, or buffet her, and load her with reproaches, for daring to survive him? She knew her Manu and her Sāstras as many of our own estimable poor know their own Holy Books, and they had taught her that great lesson of humility to man which, in the end, all such books are made to teach. " A woman is not to be relied on ”—she had the text by heart—“ a husband must be revered as a god by a virtuous wife.” Poor slaves of the slave! beautiful and tender creatures, ever the most apt in the learning of subjection! when will your turn come? Victoria, my tale is done.’

Victoria toyed with her scarf awhile as though to remember all the points, then untied it knot by knot, in sheer weariness of soul.

‘ And is that England, is that the Empire? ’ she said, fixing me with her eyes in a way I did not exactly like.

‘ Oh no, not altogether. Don't let me be unfair. There are hundreds of square miles of beauty, refinement, luxury; exquisitely ordered homes, fine-natured men, courteous, suave, poised, high-bred from the bone; white women, oh, so white! some of them able to read Greek—Learning robed and perfumed. And for parties, picture galleries, libraries, when they give their minds to such things, they are not to be matched. We are particularly proud of one square mile bounded by Oxford Street, Piccadilly, Regent Street, and

Park Lane; and are wont to repeat the boast at public dinners that, for intelligence, culture, wit, and the high qualities of civilisation, it has not its territorial equivalent on the face of the earth.'

'The greater shame for them; why do they leave the other square miles as they are?'

'There are charities, you know.'

'Charities!—ointment for a cancer. What makes the disease? There must be something going on that none of you find out. I know there must be. How can all those fine people live a day, an hour, till they do find it out? What do they talk about while they are having their dinners? I know they could find it out, if they tried. Let us try and find it out, before we go home: we have still half an hour left. I have been thinking, all the time you talked: it must be selfishness. Everybody gets what he can, instead of what he ought, and of course the clever people get most. Then they give a little of it back to the Poor Stupids in what you call charity, and go on making the money and the misery all the same. That is the way it strikes me.

How do the rich people get rich? Don't you
know you can't be rich without doing wrong,
whether you know you are doing wrong, or
not. Can you now? At the best, even, if
you are not a robber, you are using your
cleverness to take some one else's share. And
to think of all those people looking so nice,
and smelling like flowers, and talking like
expensive books, and trying to get richer than
other people all the time; oh! the sly things!
How *do* you grow rich? I wonder how it is
done.'

'Always, at the beginning, of course, by
getting as much as you can for yourself, and
giving as little as you can to others; buying
in the cheapest, and selling in the dearest is
the accepted phrase. Sometimes, this has
happened so long ago that the possessors are
able to forget it ever happened. They are
usually put up to do the talking about un-
selfishness.'

'Just what I thought; so the dealer that
buys the match boxes made in Mr. Swart's
house buys them, not for what he ought, but
for what he can.'

'Can is the only ought in practical life.'

'I see; and that makes the poor people hungry and cold.'

'I suppose so.'

'And when they are very hungry, and very cold, the dealer, and his well-to-do friends give them a little soup and a blanket.'

'That's about it.'

'Oh, how funny! how funny! how funny!'

'What would you have him do?'

'What would you?'

'I don't know.'

'You do know. Is there anything but one thing—take less himself, and give them more?'

'Then he would not be so rich as the other match box makers.'

'Well?'

'And he would have to live in a smaller house.'

'Well?'

'And give up his carriage.'

'Well?'

'Then he'll be damned if he'll do it, Vickey, so there!'

'That may be; I am only talking of what he ought to do. But I think you are wrong. He would, if he knew, only he does not know.

Perhaps the clergyman sometimes forgets to tell him. Never mind that; let us go on; it is so amusing. Tell me some other ways of making money.'

'Well, you invest in Companies, and take the profits as they come.'

'Without asking how the profits are made, how the people live that make the profits?'

'Usually so. Now and then the question is asked, but the questioner is called an eccentric. There was one shareholder that made a great fuss about the tramway people, who are worked almost into brutishness for the sake of the dividend. It was only a woman, you know; and her out-of-the-way proceeding made her quite notorious at once. The truth is, everybody feels that the poor people would grind each other just as hard, if they could.'

'Ah, the poor people would like to be just as wicked as their betters! Is that what you mean?'

'I think it is, Miss Socrates.'

'But how *do* the betters spend the money? What can be the use of it after all?'

'The use of it? Did you never hear of yachting, hunting, pretty pictures, pretty

women, good wine? Poor little savage, you
have never had so much as a taste of life!
Why you may spend twenty or thirty thousand
pounds in getting a good breed of race-horses,
if that is your hobby. You get a hobby,
that's the way it's done—horses, hounds,
women, pictures, or china. anything will do—
and keep on sinking your money till you
have the rarest and the best.'

'Is there any taste in that way as to im-
proving the breed of men? Does a rich man
ever buy a slum, and keep on playing with it
till he has turned it into a paradise?'

'No; breeding is chiefly done for the shows.'

'Are all the people in Europe as funny as
that?' said Victoria, 'or is it only the English? But see, the sun has struck the big
banyan: it is dinner time! What a lot you
have told me, but you have only told me half.
There are Rich Stupids, I see, as well as Poor
Stupids, and I think the rich ones are the
worse off.'

CHAPTER XX.

A VILLAGE FESTIVAL.

IT has never occurred to me till this moment, but certainly we two live here alone. There are a few other people on the Island, I believe, and I see them every day, but only as pictures. I talk to them too, but only as one talks to pictures, not much heeding the answer back.

I have seen the Ancient, of course, and have had many a talk with him. There are the evenings; and it is not Victoria all the time. I am one of the great family, and I come and go in that unnoticed way which is the true footing of friendship and love.

I am more particularly aware of the Ancient just now, because he is issuing a proclamation. There is to be a public holiday in celebration of the Queen's birthday, and the proclamation is to regulate the order of proceedings. It is written on a slate, and hung outside his Excellency's hut. He has been elaborating it for days, with my modest help, for the text, and Victoria's, for the common sense. Whenever we are going to do anything foolish, she interrupts from the window, where she sews by the fading light. She has thus effectually vetoed the following projects—a review of the garrison ; a banquet with speeches ; and a levée at Government House.

It is all settled now. There is to be a Spelling Bee at the school-house, followed by a lecture on the Antiquities of the Island, by the schoolmaster. The populace will then be released for Sports and Pastimes, with prizes ranging from a nosegay to a sack of potatoes. For the wind-up, there is to be another lecture, ' to steady their minds,' and I am to be the lecturer.

I fought hard against it ; I honestly did, but I was overborne. 'Something about England, sir ; we are never tired of that.' The voice from the window assented, and then I gave way.

It begins, it begins ; never mind the pre-liminaries, the blessed day is here ! *Vive la joie!* Three fowling-pieces fire a salute, the first thing in the morning, and proclaim our revel to the universe. The Union Jack is run up at the flag-staff. Our breakfasts are despatched in a few minutes, and in less than an hour we are amid the fierce excitements of the Bee.

The competition is open to all comers, but it is, in effect, confined to the younger folk. The scholars, in their best, sit at one end of the schoolroom, with the schoolmaster in front of them, to call time, and an admiring audience beyond. The severity of the struggle betokens much secret preparation. The first heat is the spelling of proper names from Scripture. ' Achaichus ' is attacked with much spirit, and carried with a shout, but we have to mourn the loss of some of our number before the flag waves over the conquered word. ' Achaicharus ' yields in time, though it leaves but few survivors of a forlorn hope. ' Habaziniah ' covers the field with slain, yet still we win. ' Geuel,' owing to some invincible difficulty in the placing of the vowels, plunges many of the competitors into tears. ' Gezerites ' restores us all to good humour with a sense of universal failure. We cannot manage the final ' s,' where it is emphatic—a disability common to all our Island folk.

I pass over the other heats, to come to that lecture on Antiquities. Like the memorable trial, it is a function held in the open air. We break up the Bee, and troop forth, the man of learning at our head, and examine a few huge flat stones, which we have seen a hundred times before. They are the gravestones of our pre-historic race. There is one in front of a cottage, whither it has been removed to make a flag-stone for the porch. Another lies, where the vanished men left it, in a field on the other side of the Ridge. We know what we should find beneath, if we took it up—a human skeleton sleeping the long sleep, with a pearl shell for a pillow. For centuries it has slept there ; for centuries let it sleep on. We cross the Ridge again, to the Peak where I first met Victoria ; and we are told to look for the traces of four rude stone figures that once stood there on a platform, as though to keep eternal watch upon the sea. Most of us have seen these traces from our earliest infancy, but we look for them again with great diligence, and communicate the result with the cries appropriate to sudden and unexpected discovery—all to please the schoolmaster. We ask how they came there? what they signify?—'tis a part of the game. We are told that they afford undoubted evidence of a remoter Island race. But how did the race reach the Island? The lecturer bids us guess. Is there one of us so ill-bred as to hazard the suggestion of a boat? Not one! We play out our honest piece honestly, to the last scene. We hold our tongues: our virtue, or our habit, or verbal veracity will not allow us to do more. A rosy brown infant, who cries ' I know,' is hustled to the rear by Victoria, and has his mouth stopped with an orange. For that matter, the whole comedy is devoid of guile.

The lecturer knows that we might all echo the cry of the infant; only he must have an opening for his line :—' How about a raft from the Gambier Islands, three hundred miles away?' ' Ah, yes, a raft to be sure! But then, why should they come here?' It is impossible to deny him that. ' Suppose they came because they couldn't help it,' returns the man of lore. 'That would certainly alter the case. But how?' He needs no more. 'In earlier times, especially, and even within living memory, it was the custom of the rude natives of the South Pacific to put their vanquished enemies on a raft, and commit them to the mercy of the waves.' There is more of it, but this may serve.

'Come, and I will show you something,' says the good man; and we follow him again —this time down the steep path to the market grove, and up the other steep path to the settlement, and through the settlement, till we stop at his own cottage door, and come to a final halt in his bedroom, which is the museum of the Island. What matter, if we have already seen the solitary shelf that holds the entire national collection! What matter, if these spear heads and axe heads of stone are only less familiar to the hand than our own knives and forks! We are doing a fellow-creature a kindness—that is enough. And the way of doing it is so pleasant to ourselves! It is the ideal combination duty and delight. For, that walk to the museum was a walk through the fields of Paradise, with bare-

legged children for attendant angels, fleet as
any shapes with wings. Behind these, the
bigger lads and lasses, too old for play, too
young for love, trod the rock, as though it
were soft cloud, in the lightness of their
perfect strength. And behind them, man and
maiden, maiden and man, dragged the slow
foot of the deepest spiritual joy. May the
time be far distant when they, too, shall sleep
on the pearl shell!

I have forgotten all about my lecture,
until the schoolmaster reminds me of it. at
the conclusion of his own. He uses the
freedom of a brother artist to make a
courteous inquiry as to my choice of a topic,
and I am obliged to confess that no thought
of preparation for the coming duty has once
entered my mind. 'We shall expect you to
do your best for us,' he says, with a smile.
'I could not venture to do less,' is my answer.
'after what I have just heard.' But this, like
most smooth sayings, leaves us just where we
were. I begin to cast about for a theme.
'I have seen your festival; how would you
like to hear of a festival on a larger scale,
on the other side of the world? " A

Roman Holiday "—what do you think of that ? '

' But you said you would tell us something about England.'

' I mean a holiday in modern Rome ; and modern Rome, you know, is on the banks of the Thames.'

' That would do perfectly. Would you like to sit in my bedroom, and collect your thoughts ? '

' He will collect nothing there, but stones and bones,' says Victoria, who has lingered with us. ' He wants watching, if you are to get any work out of him. Nobody can manage him, but me. Come, sir, come along ! '

One may be in leading like a bear, or like a man of genius ; and I hope I am not a bear. My leader makes straight for the Peak, by the grove sacred to her tenderest thoughts. She establishes me on the ruins of the platform, solitary now, for it will not be the scene of a lecture for another year. As she leaves me, I receive the order to remain perfectly still, in profitable meditation, until her return. I promise, and I perform. I throw myself down on my back, watch the floating billions of light globules that seem to make the substance of the air, and wonder if each of them, all proportions preserved, holds a divine Victoria, and a contemplative Me. What a conception of the infinite in happiness, if it could be so! Then, anon, a light footstep warns me that she is here again ; and I leave all speculation for the sweet and sufficient certainty that the larger globule holds us two. She has a basket of fruit in her hand; but is it Flora or is it Minerva? The emblems are confusing, for a pencil and a little note-book lie on the top of the store. The bananas and the guavas are to make a lunch for the lonely thinker; the pencil and the paper are to preserve his precious thoughts for the lecture, ere they fly away. I stretch out an eager hand for the eatables, but she offers me the pencil first.

'Put down what you have been thinking about while I was away.'

How doubly delicious it would be if there were but a shade of coquetry in it ; but there is not—not the shadow of a shade.

'I have been thinking about the Infinite.'

'What a waste of time!   I thought it was to be about Roman Holidays.'

'It!   What?   Oh, the lecture.   Yes.'

'Do you mean to say you have not been—oh, how lazy you are!'

'And how silly, you, my Victoria! but I like you best that way.'

'What have I to do with it?'

'So much that, without you, the whole world——'

'Will you eat a banana?'

'I do not mind, if you will eat one too.'

'I have no appetite.'

'Nor I.'

'You seemed quite hungry just now.'

'So I was.'

She was kneeling with the basket before her, and she began to straighten her shape, always, with her, a sign of a certain concentration of feeling.   But she still retained her posture, and she looked like a fragment of a grand statue, broken short off at the hem of the robe.

'Don't you think you are a little uncertain in your sayings and doings, sometimes?   If you are hungry, why won't you eat?'

‘ It is a hunger strike.’

‘ What is that ? ’

‘ An invention of the Siberian captives. When they are very sick of everything, they strike against their dinners, and die.’

‘ You need not starve yourself to get anything in our gift,’ she said, and her glance intensified the grave beauty of her face.

It was too delicious ; who could have helped going on ?

‘ Yes, I know ; I have everything, and still I want one thing more.’

‘ Oh, now I understand,’ she said, rising to her full height, and making a great litter of fruit and writing materials, as she overturned the basket. ‘ Oh, I understand perfectly ; I know exactly what you want to say. You need not go on with your half meanings, in that sly way. You said it once before, and you promised you would never say it again.’

Silly Victoria, she has spread all the cards on the table, and killed the game ! One short half-hour’s lesson in a London boudoir, for that matter, in a London schoolroom, would have taught her how to play. This comes of being brought up to tell the truth like a Quaker, by an Ancient in a savage isle.

'All the same, Victoria, I won't eat my lunch.'

'Dear friend, dear, dear friend, if I might only say to you all I want to say ! But why do you trouble me so, why do you try to make me do wrong ? '

It was my turn to jump up now, and to take her hand, which she did not refuse.

' Victoria, who can contend against you ? You play by your own rules, and mine seems the sharper's game. Come, the hunger strike is over ; hand up the fruit.'

Victoria peeled the bananas, and I ate them. This arrangement was nearly as good as the best. It was glorious sunshine again in her face, as in the sky above. 'Not more than others I deserve, yet God hath given me more,' was my humble grace.

By-and-by, but all too soon, I was left to my reflections once more. Victoria withdrew, on the understanding that I should work at my lecture during her absence. I watched her to the foot of the slope, fixing myself in an attitude of meditation when she turned to watch me. I saw her skirmishing with a band of infant wanderers who wanted to climb to my study, and heading them off, with much ingenuity, into an orchard beyond the Ridge.

I really tried to work, but it was impossible. The sounds and sights of the fête came up to me, on my lofty post of observation, from all the peopled region of the Isle, and from the more distant summits on the other side, that rose like towers from the wall of rock. Distance subdued every laugh and shout, every cry of bird or beast, into perfect harmony with the rhythmic beat of the waves ; and the sounds seemed but varied modes of musical silence. There was the same harmony in the tints, seen through the wide stretches of summer mist. It was sometimes almost impossible to say where the flowers ended, and the men and women began. You might tell it only by the motion of the figures darting in and out of the patches of blossom, as pursuers and pursued. The pairs that sauntered soon became absolutely one with the landscape, as they moved further from the point of view. It was exquisite to the sense and to the soul, as an image of the unity of nature. Sky and earth and sea, man and woman, flower and tree, seemed but so many forms and manifestations of one universal element of beauty, each separate perception of the beholder realising them in a uniform impression, in its own way. I was busy with this fancy, face downwards in the grass, and trying to work it out in consultation with a wild-flower, when Victoria surprised me again. If she had sought my life, it would have been hers, for she was within a yard of me, before I knew that she was there.

'Princess, hear my confession before you begin to frown. I have done nothing; nothing—nothing done! Now I *will* begin, just whenever you like. Only I cannot work here; I must go somewhere else.'

'Home to your own room?'

'Stuffy!'

'Where then?' Tapping the turf carpet with her naked foot.

'I know; only I mustn't say.'

'Just say it out.'

'To the Cave; the Cave of the Great Scrape, where we went before.'

‘ Madness ! You’ll just be killed, if you try it.’

‘ Was I killed the first time ? ’

‘ I helped you.’

‘ I want you to help me again.’

‘ I wonder why I like you at all, and I do like you so much.’ Then, after a pause, ‘ If God meant to let you be killed, He would never make me help to do it. Come along.’

This feat of engineering having been once described, the courteous reader may wish to be spared the repetition of its details. It is enough to say that I was soon walking along the narrow ridge, with my eyes closed, by order, and with my hands on the shoulders of Victoria, who led the way. Just before the eyes closed, they caught one look of tenderest concern in hers that was a thing to remember for a lifetime. When I was allowed to open them again, we were both in the Cave. Victoria left, the moment she saw me safe, promising to come back in an hour, and fetch me out.

CHAPTER XXI.

A ROMAN HOLIDAY.

I WAS alone with the clouds, the ocean, and
my note-book. I could attend to the note-
book, only by forgetting the ocean and the
clouds; so, after one last look at them, I
retired to the back of the Cave, and set to
work.

NOTES FOR THE LECTURE.

'*Old England and Old Rome; Parallel.*—
England, my friends, you are to understand,
is in the position of Old Rome after the
conquest. She is sitting down to enjoy the
world she has won. She wants no more:
after dinner, the lion would not hurt a fly.
She feels the lassitude of digestion, especially
in governing circles. Yet, somehow, the
duties of empire are still carried on. Rome
fed all her children from the subject realms,
and they all grew lazy. England feeds only

some of hers, and, what with need and hunger, the watch of empire is duly kept. The reliefs are sent out to the distant provinces: the pro-consuls come home regularly to die of liver-complaint in ancestral halls. Take a bird's-eye view of our hemisphere, and you would see its main roads of earth and ocean speckled with the foam or dust that marks the movements of her legions. 'Tis a pretty sight!

'*Holiday Preparations.*—The public holidays in England are ordained by law, and, three or four times a year, there is a general suspension of work in this workshop of the world. It is a Sabbath of popular festivity. One of its first signs is the general migration from town of the select few. All who can possibly manage it get out of the way—only, of course, to leave more room for the others. It is just like them.

'London is given up to its masses, with all its spacious environs. The streets are theirs, the parks are theirs. Every lamp-post in the slums is turned into a screw swing.

'*Adaptiveness of the Race.*—The diversions of infancy among the English masses are of primitive simplicity. The youthful slummer plays, as the mature savage wrought, with the rudest tools. His swing is the knotted fragment of a clothes-line; and, in the national game, he demands no more than a bundle of old coats for the wicket, with a splinter of deal for the bat. This healthy contempt for " plant " shows the adaptiveness of the race, its readiness in making the most of the materials that come to hand. Waterloo was won in the playing fields of Eton, and Australia in the playing fields of Seven Dials. Walk through St. James's Park on a public holiday, and you can no longer doubt it. Cricket is contrived with the implements aforesaid; football, with an old hat, or a broken kettle. The same adaptiveness is shown in all the arrangements: the average of breech, to the extent of nakedness it has to cover, may be put at about three-fifths. Yet there are no glaring whites to mar the beauty of the landscape; and even the faces are in a sort of keeping of pale green. Artists might picture this Bank Holiday scene in the Park ; it could hardly fail to attract attention at Burlington House. The sicklier children,

and the very young, play in the alleys nearer
home, where the dust is considerately left in
sufficient abundance to enable them to make
their mud-pies. Many play in the old grave-
yards adjacent to these alleys, recently opened
to them by the munificence of a public-
spirited society. This is perhaps the highest
example of our national readiness to make
the best of circumstances.

' *Note.*—Sketch of Tom All Alone's—real
or supposed—on a public holiday, as one of
the most suggestive sights of the universe:
"Tom All Alone's; with a few observations
on Russell Court and Vinegar Yard." Ancient
cemetery or native barrow of district, consist-
ing of three back-yards rolled into one; now
a public playground, dedicated for ever, etc.,
with becoming circumstance, as local " boon."
To get it into focus, should be seen from the
meadows about Eton College. So seen, will
inspire sentiments of devout gratitude to God
for the mysteries of patience, far surpassing
the mysteries of faith, in the souls of men.
Tom All Alone's, as something to be thankful
for. Ha! ha! ha! (try to laugh here). Oh,
by what magic, by what magic, do we get

them to take this irreducible minimum in settlement of the human claim? (try not to weep).

'Same adaptability, too, in grown-up natives of region—veritable note of our race. Require no costly machinery of enjoyment. Take a plank of wood, put a row of taps and glasses on one side, and, on the other, a kind of horse box in which fifteen or twenty people may manage to stand upright, and you have " house of entertainment." A young woman turns taps, as fast as she can, and fills glasses ; people in horse-box empty them with equal dispatch ; and public enjoyment is at its height. Marble tables, public gardens, flowers, music, not indispensable. A trough would be simpler still ; but horses do not care for gin, and the higher animal would object to it, as it implies the unsound principle of community of goods.

'Here, in these houses of entertainment, they exchange their artless confidences, and settle their family affairs. Not inquisitive about future; have learned to take short views. Whenever perplexed about problems of destiny, and their own relations of joy to this joyous world, they nod to young woman, who turns tap, and their perplexities disappear.

' *Note.*—The beautiful modesty of their demand on life might teach even shepherds a lesson in content. Their simple attainable standard in wine, in woman, in music, in light, in joy. Their conversation—direct and plain, free from tortuous refinements of studied wit; their badinage, usually no more than the light play of the pewter on one another's heads. All their pleasures of the same simple description. Will spend their leisure very contentedly in watching a dog worrying a pitfull of rats, or two men beating each other into insensibility with gloves that only seem to hurt. As childlike as the North American Indians, and not unlike them in the race type—high cheek bones; a wide mouth, massively lipped; slits for the eyes. See them on the great public days. pouring out in myriads to a horse race, boat race, or Lord Mayor's Show; and own the wonders of a social and religious system that has suffered them to find satisfaction in this state, or us to find content.

' Amplify admiration of the system, in the lyric vein—rhythmic prose, etc.

' *Their Women.*—Like their North American sisters, fond of feathers and bright hues. No gaudier thing in nature than the coster girl in her holiday dress of mauve, with the cruel plume that seems to have been dyed in blood. Relation of female to male, singular survival of primitive state. Love-making always, in form at least, an abduction of the virgin. A meeting at the street corner in the dusk, for the beginning of the ceremony; then a chase round the houses, the heavy boots after the light ones, with joyous shrieks to mark the line of flight; after that, the seizure, the fight, with sounding slaps for dalliance that might knock the wind out of a farrier of the Blues. In the final clutch, skirts part in screeching rents, feathers strew the ground. Then the panting pair return, hand in hand, to the street corner, to begin again.

' *A Night Piece.*—Nightfall brings the whole slum together, at the universal rendez-vous, from every near or distant scene; men, and those that were once maidens, mumbling

age and swearing infancy, stand six-deep before
the slimy bar, till the ever flowing liquor
damps down their fiercest fires, and the great
city is once more at rest. The imagination of
him that saw Hell could hardly picture the
final scene.'

.   .   .   .   .   .

'Are you ready?'

The voice came from the rock above, and
it was hers.

'Yes, pining for liberty—please let me
out.'

'Have you done your work?'

'Yes.'

'Word of honour?'

'Word of honour!'

'I am coming—you may come and look
at me, if you like ; but mind : don't you try
to look down.'

I walked to the mouth of the Cave, and
there, a few yards above me, was the beautiful
head peeping over the summit, the eyes smiling
down into mine. Only the face was visible ;
she must have been stretched full length on
the rock.

A few moments, and I was in soft delicious

touch of her again, as we crept along the ledge ;
and I kept touch, as we crossed the angle of
the slope on our way to the schoolhouse, for,
though help was no longer needed, Victoria
still let me guard her hand. And so we
walked through the twilight, without wanting
to speak a word.

That lecture was never delivered. When
I saw all their happy faces in the schoolroom,
I felt that I could not spoil their holiday. I
accordingly chose another subject, while the
Ancient was making his introductory speech,
and trusted to my star. The star was friendly.
The Ancient wasted a good deal of time ;
and, when he sat down, I was ready for a
spirited improvisation on the Benefits of the
Printing Press, with which they were perfectly content.

'Light the torches, Reuben,' said the old
man when the applause had subsided, 'and
let the youngsters go bird-nesting on the
Ridge, for the wind-up. Victoria, and all the
girls that are good girls, will stay behind and
sing us a song. There is light enough on the
Green.'

CHAPTER XXII.

MISUNDERSTANDING.

A QUARREL with Victoria?—no, not a quarrel, I want another word. Only 'a something.' What is it? I do not know.

Victoria has become 'unaccountable'—we will put it in that way. There is no knowing what to be at with Victoria: the grievance is there. And 1 have tried so hard to find out.

That affair of the Peak was a lesson, or I tried to make it one. 'Leave Victoria alone,' it seemed to say, 'and keep your homage, respectful and other, to yourself. Victoria wants to tell you something, but does not know how to begin. Cannot you save her the trouble? You confuse her with your homage, respectful and other, and she wants you to leave her alone. Curly stops the way.

'What matter that Curly is as vague as something in Orion! He has taken her heart with him into space. Leave her alone.

'Do you want further proof of it? How many more times must you see her prostrate before his shrine in the thicket, as you saw her yesterday, when you dogged her footsteps like a spy? How many more times must you hear her cry, "Come back, come back, and help me!" between her passionate kisses of the bits of fetich on the boughs?

'And, if there were no Curly, how would that avail? Victoria is not for you. Are you to stay here for ever? You know you are not. And how could you take Victoria away?

'Victoria is a savage; and who would have her anything else? Will you put Pocahontas in crêpe de Chine and surah, in lace, embroideries, and gimp, and transplant her to the London drawing-rooms, to make sport for the London crowd? Are you looking forward to this: "A lady whose tall figure is well known in London society wore black silk, opening over a front of white silk muslin, draped from neck to feet, and confined at the waist with a pointed band of black velvet, fastened by a diamond clasp "?

' It will not do.

' Friendship is impossible on your side: when you are with her, you invariably play the fool. Keep out of her way.'

So, I am no longer Victoria's shadow. I wander alone. I make up to the Ancient, and borrow his fowling piece, to pay my respects to the wild birds. The wild birds do not mind. I trouble them a good deal less than I trouble Victoria. It is an old fowling piece; how did men contrive to kill anything in the days when it was made, especially to kill one another? The slaughter of Malplaquet quite enhances one's respect for the race, and takes rank with Stonehenge and the Pyramids among material marvels wrought by simple means.

I have kept this up for some days, and I am popping at a flock of gulls this morning, with so slight a breach of the good understanding between us that the flock increases, by the effect of intelligent curiosity, as the sport goes on, when Victoria stands between me and the light.

It is here that Victoria begins to be unaccountable: on the strength of this incident, I made the charge.

For Victoria has come to look for me. There is no need to guess it: she says so in terms. Only mark what follows this admission, and say if I am without a grievance.

'Why have you come to look for me, Victoria?'

'I am so miserable.'

'Why?'

'You make me miserable.'

'What have I done, Princess?'

'What have *I* done? You have hardly spoken to me for three days.'

'I thought you would like that best, Victoria.'

'Why should you think so? What would this place be to me, if we were bad friends?'

'I trouble you.'

'Leave me to judge of that. There cannot be any harm in seeing you, in talking to you.'

So, I leave the disgusted gulls; and we ramble to the further side of the Island, to the place where I landed in the dawn of history to find the New World.

We do not talk much at first. I am working out the situation, with due aid from certain phrases of convention that help to reconcile poverty of thought to self-respect. These little felicities of epigram on the inconsistency of Woman never helped anybody to comprehension of her; yet, if they were taken out of its phrase books, the world would be acutely sensible of the void. Few people are inconsistent, but a good many people fail to understand. I wish I were not so dull. I seem to have found Victoria to about as much purpose as a savage might find a watch.

So, for some precious moments, it is the old footing again. We are as free as the other animals about us, and perhaps still more exquisitely happy. It might be rash, though, to attempt to answer for any but ourselves. Our myriads of birds and insects, and our select assortment of beasts, seem to have a good time—a life in the sun, and a quick death in their prime of strength, with their business hours mainly employed in dining, and in exercise in the open air. Most of the beasts belong to the Island family as much as the men and women; and Victoria could give them each a name. With her, they only play at being wild; and the outlaw goats seek her as regularly for their morning caress as their friends who have made their peace with civilisation.

If she and I could be like this for ever! But we cannot. We seem to be friends and strangers, by turns; for the life of me, I know not why. We move to and from each other in some mysterious way. For, what happened just now, happens again and again. I am with her, as I could always wish to be, till some subtle change in her manner makes me think she wants me to keep away. I keep away, and she seeks me out, with reproaches for coldness and neglect. We reach perfection, and then imperfection begins. Slowly, slowly, as some change in the colour of a plant, comes Victoria's new mistrust of me, or of herself. What is it? what can it be? It is a movement of some strange law of her emotions; but what is the law? The savage has learned so much about his watch as to feel the utter inadequacy of the reflection that watches have curious ways. He cannot examine, but he begins to guess. There is

but one guess to make, the old one—it must
be the phantasm of the living Curly that
stands between us and the perfect light. We
know what came of that guess before. If I
step back to make way for him, Victoria will
follow, to know the reason why. A pest on
him for a phantom that plays us on and off:
it is neither my fault, nor Victoria's; it is the
phantom that does not know its own mind!

CHAPTER XXIII.

ANOTHER SAIL.

LET him be forgotten for the moment. There is a new ship off the Point!

Not an English ship this time—a Yankee, by her beautiful flag.

It is the old scene—the hurried assembling of the people; the signals and answering signals; the manning of the surf boat; the meeting of the elders for consultation as to ways and means of reception. But this meeting is for serious work. The new ship is a trader; and only a ship of war imports no danger to these defenceless folk. There may be a rough crew, not too well in hand, fierce men, beyond punishment for excess, immediate or remote. If they choose to go wrong, the whole Island is at their mercy, not only in goods and chattels, but in the honour of the women, the lives of all.

The troubled Ancient, I think, would like to bury his treasure of maidens for awhile, if only he might hope to dig them up again, safe and sound, when the danger is past. He looks about him with the furtive glance that seeks a hiding-place, like some Jute progenitor on the approach of a pirate horde. But he wisely gives no public sign of alarm, and he sets out in his whaler to board the new-comer, with a cheerful face.

All depends upon the character of the Captain, and we are re-assured upon that point the moment he steps ashore. He gives a 'candy' from his pocket to a child, and lifts his hat to one of the girls in a way that is unmistakeable as a sign of genuine respect.

He is unlike all other sea captains, past and present, if not to come. He is a young, blonde dandy, with his hair parted in the middle, regular features, and a silken moustache. These appearances would be altogether difficult to harmonise with his functions, but for the firm set of the lips, and the glance of the clear blue eye. His handkerchief is slightly scented—there cannot be a doubt of it. and he is above the suspicion of a quid.

His speech sometimes betrays his origin, but does not, in the least, betray his calling. He 'shivers' no 'timbers'—but none of them ever do that. He occasionally talks like a book, and rather like a book read aloud in class. This, however, is only when he has time to think of himself, and to behave at his best. At these moments, happily rare, his construction is anything but idiomatic; it is classically ornate. The Americanism appears in his puritanical anxiety to give every word, and every letter of every word, its full phonetic value. He extends the principles of the Declaration of Independence to his syllables, and makes them all free and equal, without a trace of accentuation that might render one the tyrant of the rest. His orthoepic constitution for the language, in short, is a constitution without a king. Yet he has the fear of Webster ever before his eyes, and that authority is evidently his Supreme Court.

We lodge him in our house, at my request. This, I believe, anticipates a desire of the Ancient, who, while awaiting fuller knowledge, wants to have him under his eye. He shares

my chamber, and is accommodated with a
spare bed therein.   His crew, with one or two
exceptions, abide on the ship, but they have
shore leave, and, before they have it, so says
the Ancient, who brought him off, he makes
them a short speech, which is evidently
remembered throughout their entire stay.   He
is a restless man.   Almost as soon as he takes
up his quarters under our roof, he leaves them ;
and, before sundown, he has walked all over
the Island ; has inquired into its systems of
government, laws, agriculture, commerce, and
manufactures ; has recognised the clock as a
gift from Chicago, the organ as a present from
Salem ; and has suggested improvements in
nearly every process of industry, that would
double the yield.   He has also asked to see
our newspaper ; and, without waiting to learn
that we do not possess such a thing, has offered
us a bundle of journals of both hemispheres
which, he says, may supply ' items ' of interest
for the compilation of the local sheet.

At first he was taciturn, or merely interro-
gatory ; and he showed extreme caution in his
communications to us.   But, towards evening,
all this disappeared, and his fluency, and

readiness to relate his own story left nothing to be desired.

It was the typical American career of the past, and so, for all his freshness and alertness, I thought him an old-fashioned man. The new generation of Americans are mostly men of one career, as we are : this one was of half a dozen. He had begun life as an office boy, had been a real-estate agent, a lawyer, an editor of a newspaper, and was now a skipper, by what he considered a process of quite orderly development. He had sailed from San Francisco, and he was going to make the tour of the world, by way of Suez and the Mediterranean, Liverpool and New York. His ship was his own property, and her cargo was his pocket-money for the voyage. The Ancient asked him how he learned the trade of the sea, but he seemed unaware that there was a trade to learn. He could hardly remember a time when he did not know it, in its elements. As a boy, he used to sail a yacht about New York Bay ; and he had served a year in a whaler, before the mast. At one time, he had thought of going into art.

How had he learned editing, then ? That,

too, he hardly knew. All crafts, he assured us, were governed by the same general principle of common sense. Editing a newspaper was but sailing a ship, under new conditions. You put your mind to it, and you rounded your back for the burden of your inevitable mistakes. If he had a natural turn, he thought, it was for scheming things, and getting down to first principles. In the course of his journalistic experiences, it had once been his duty to turn out a weekly column of jokes. He was not a joker by taste, nor by choice, but he could invent jokes, of course, if it had to be done. He studied out the principles of the thing, and he found that they lay in startling contrasts, and in startling similitudes. With a little practice, he soon became able to make a joke on anything—the inkstand on his desk, the rent in the carpet, the passing shower. He settled the points beforehand, and then worked up to them, straight and sharp. The failures came from ' fooling around' the subject. He made two or three jokes for us, as specimens. He did this with a perfectly grave face, apologising for a certain rustiness of habit due to his having been for some time out of that line. They were really very fair jokes; and, if we had not been so fully forewarned of the expected result, I think we might have laughed. They had to be 'popped' on you, as he explained. The Ancient promised to try them on Reuben, and our new acquaintance warranted they would make him gay. On the same general principle of observation, he had invented a way of simplifying a ship's rig, saving 45 per cent. in cordage and blocks; and he promised to show us a model of it, made on the voyage.

By nightfall, we felt that he had exhausted us and our little island, and that he would fain be off. This, however, was impossible for the moment: the ship wanted more fresh provisions, and she was, besides, under slight repairs. It fretted him sorely, for he could not be still. Never did I see such feverish activity, such a passion for doing something. His meals were a mockery of Divine Providence; but, as he did not choke, he must have been reserved for special uses. In ten minutes he had disposed of fish, flesh, and his hunk of pie. Only a Rabelais could conceive the war of elements within. There was no rest in him, nor near him; he was busy all over the surface of life, with no sense of the true uses of any one thing. It was a sheer fury of industrial action, like the old Berserker fury of war. He worked for the love of it, as the children of Starkader fought; and he seemed to have no more profit of his labour than they of their shedding of blood. It seemed quite a triumph to get him to bed.

He slept in my room, as I have said, or he was to sleep. But he could not lay him down till he had analysed the composition of the mattress, and thrown out suggestions for a new kind of stuffing, to be made of something that grew wild at the foot of the Peak. In the midst of his discourse on this point, he fell asleep, as suddenly as though he had turned himself off at the main. I, too, dropped off in a few minutes, and I slept soundly for a few hours, until I was awakened, long before dawn, by the gleam of a candle in my eyes.

He, of course, had lit the candle; and he was sitting upright in bed, and peering intently, through an eyeglass, at something which he held betwixt his finger and thumb.

'See here,' he said, without any apology for waking me ; ' if that don't beat all ! '

' What is it ? ' I asked in some alarm.

' Just the strongest moth you ever saw in your life—pulls like a little cart-horse. I was lighting-up for a bit of quiet thinking, and in he buzzed.'

' Let him go again.'

' Oh, he can go : I shan't want him yet,' and he flung the insect off. ' Are there many of his sort here, I wonder ? We must ask old Forelock,' so he called our host.

' What if there are ? '

' See here,' he said, propping himself up with his pillow, and, to my dismay, preparing for a long talk. ' See here : I'll tell you something ; that insect is undeveloped Power.'

' Well, what of that ? '

' Can't you see ? ' he asked in a tone expressive of his certainty that I could not.

I gave him the desired negative, and he went on.

' That insect means half the motive power in Nature clean thrown away.'

' I do not follow you, as yet.'

‘ I dare say, but you will come to it. How
about all the beasts of the field and the rest
of them being created for the service of
man ? ’

‘ How about it ! ’ I was still only half
awake.

‘ Well, they skulk their work, that’s all.
Half of them do nothing for their keep ; do
you begin to follow me now ? ’

‘ How should they ? ’

‘ Set them to work ; that’s the idea.’

I was wide awake now. It seemed like
a disclosure of some new invention in crime ;
and, so far, it was appropriate to the midnight hour, the darkness, and the deadly quiet
of the scene.

‘ You surely never mean to say that you
want to put the song birds into factories ? ’

‘ That is just what I do mean. It is only
a fad of mine at present, but I shall work it
out to something by-and-by. Did you ever
see the performing fleas ? ’

‘ No ; it is the only thing I have not seen.’

‘ Well, sir, I have, and, from that moment,
I was a changed man. It is a mere toy with
the showmen ; to a man that can put two and

two together, it is what the fall of the apple was to Newton. The first time I saw it, I did not sleep for three nights. I went into a dime show in Broadway, and there were these things, along with a Circassian lady, and, I believe, a calculating boy. I began with the fleas, and I never gave another thought to the rest. There were a dozen of them, of various sizes and nationalities—English fleas, Russian fleas, American, and so on ; and there was a good deal of patter, that meant nothing, as to what each nationality could do, all winding up, of course, in honour of the Stars and Stripes. The Russian flea was big, but lazy ; the English flea tough, but obstinate ; the American flea all sprightliness, audacity, energy, and good sense. I soon stopped that, by making believe I was a Scotchman, when he produced a creature from its bed of wadding in a pill-box, and said it came from Mull, and was the smartest thing in his stables. I gave him a dollar, and asked him not to play the fool, and he fell to business at once. I wanted to get at the principle of the thing, you understand. The creatures were harnessed with a woman's hair—a man's would

have been too coarse—tied round that dip in
their bodies that makes a natural waist.
Then, when you had them fast in this way by
one end of the hair, you put the other end to
whatever you wanted to set going—Queen
Victoria's coach, in cardboard, or the miller's
cart. The flea naturally tried to get away,
and that was your motive power. When you
wanted him to turn the treadmill, you put
him up against the wheel, just like his betters
and, the faster he tried to run away, the
faster the thing went round. That was
always the principle of it; utilise the movement of flight—a new escapement beyond anything in the watchmaker's art. Well, sir, this
showman saw nothing beyond his fleas, but, at
a glance, I saw ahead of them to all animal
life. Make the animals earn their living, I
said to myself; work up your reflex action
for the benefit of man. It would solve the
labour problem: no more strikes! When
once I had got my thoughts in that groove, I
seemed to see nothing but loafing idleness in
all Nature. Take even the working animals ;
what do many of them do for Man ? There's
nothing serious in beaver dams, for instance,

from that point of view. They are generally a mere obstruction, for want of an intelligent foreman of the works. And as for the ants, though I admit they are too small to count in business, why flatter them up? I say nothing of their useless fighting; but did an ant ever make anything to eat, or anything to wear? There, sir, when I got that idea into my head, I couldn't read the poets, for sheer disgust at the way in which they wrote about these creatures, and missed the real point. It was the same when I went to a menagerie, and I always went when I could. It made me real sad. Think of the waste of power in a cage of apes! Nothing to be done with them but nut-cracking, and swinging on the horizontal bar—never tell me!'

He had now settled himself for a long night's talk, and, all things considered, I was not loath to find him a listener. There might be still more in it, I thought, than even he perceived; and, as he had looked beyond the showman, others, who were not without a lingering tenderness for a beauty of life fast perishing of the malady of use, might look beyond him. Besides, now that one was fairly

awake, it was so sweet to feel alive again.
For, beyond the gleam of his candle, I caught
a glimpse of the starry sky, and his mono-
tone was sometimes tempered to the ear by
the note of a night bird.

The bird seemed to put him in a rage.
'Just so! Just so!' he said with severity,
apostrophising the unseen musician through
the open casement. 'How should you know
better, when those who ought to know have
been encouraging you all their lives? Did
you ever read a book called "The Birds of
the Poets," my friend? It is just heartbreak-
ing, if you take it from the point of view of
an employer of labour. All this singing—
why do they do it? Just because there's
nobody to set them to work. Who does
most whistling? The loafer at the street
corner. It's pent up energy, sir, that must
find a vent. That's why there's so much fuss
about feathered love-making : they've got to
kill time. Develop industry, and you'll soon
have less billing and cooing. Look at Spain
and Italy—why it was nothing but that sort
of thing till they went into manufactures.
There ain't much guitar playing in Catalonia

now ; and you'd better not go to Bilbao, if you've a taste for the castanets. Men have got to keep themselves employed ; and, if they are not making cottons, or smelting iron, they'll be fighting duels, or running off with one another's wives. The animal kingdom is full of wasted power, that's my point. You can't use all of it : we haven't got to that pitch of intelligence ; but you can begin to try. Did you ever notice a cloud hanging low over the water, not a yard away, and stretching, perhaps, for miles and miles? What do you think it is? Young shrimps bounding up and down, just to show they're glad — millions, billions, trillions of 'em. There's power for you, if you could work it up. I don't say you could, in this case ; I don't want to be fanciful. I only say what a fine thing, if you could : let us talk like practical men. See how the dog has sneaked out of industry. One time he used to earn his own dinner by roasting his master's ; but that's all over now. I don't say he costs less than the roasting-jack, but I'm talking of the principle of the thing. What is he now? A machine for licking the hand of his owner,

and for barking when visitors pull the bell.
It ain't as though he washed your hand—
you've got to wash it after him, instead—and
if the help is too deaf to hear the bell, she
will be too deaf to hear the dog. The dog is
a humbug, and his show of affection is only a
way of fooling us out of a free lunch. What
does it amount to—all this running to and fro
after nothing, and all this jumping about?
Sheer waste of power. The Dutchmen and
the Esquimaux are the only wise people; they
turn it to account. Put him in harness, and
he'll soon leave off pawing your pants. As
for cats, I am ashamed of them, and I am
more ashamed of the human beings that
encourage them in their profitless ways. In
most houses, they don't even catch the mice :
it's all done with traps. A pet animal of any
kind is an economic monstrosity. Do you
know how I interpret the singing of birds in
their cages? They are sniggering at man to
think they have done him out of their board.
There's a use for everything; why, even
tortoises, if you know how to manage them,
will tell you when it's going to rain. Sir, I
want to make idleness a caution to the whole

animal creation—even a caution to snakes. The bloodhound—send him back into the Police service, and give him a blue overcoat for uniform, if you like. There's power everywhere; why you've a perfect sledge hammer in every alligator's tail! How about the weight of the hippopotamus for crushing cane? I'd just turn your Zoological Gardens into a factory, by thunder I would! and make every blessed animal do something for his living. No song, no supper. The squirrels would do for thread winders; the giraffes, for reaching things off shelves. You'd lose by it at starting, just as you do by prison labour, but you'd soon find out how to make it pay.'

He seemed to be growing drowsy, but I was wakeful enough, and I wanted him to go on. My curiosity seemed to gratify him, and he roused himself for a further effort.

'You want to begin somewhere, on a small scale—in some place where there's nobody to laugh. It's like any other experiment; you'll have to play with it at first, and keep your own counsel. You want a little place up in a corner; this place would do. Why not this place, eh?' he said, sitting bolt upright, and fixing me with the inventor's eye. ' You are quiet ; you are out of the world ; you ain't of much account in creation—you know my meaning—and you've no character to lose. Just think of it ; one fine day you might send your little specimen of animal manufactures to a European Exhibition, and then you'd be a second hub of the universe. What do you do with your goats, for instance? Why not put 'em into harness ? I mean real business, not baby play. How about a goat tramway from old Forelock's house there, all along the Ridge, to the foot of the Point? fare, a potato, if you must carry your small change about in that way. You are just teeming with life, sir, and life is power. Your sea birds—it's a sad sight! I know something could be done with 'em. Train up a happy family, new style—a happy factory, the whole lot, cat, and dog, and mouse, and guinea-pig, and barn-door fowl, all at work, instead of sitting on the mope, and all turning out something that would sell by the yard. Then lecture on the utilisation of reflex action all through the States. It would make your fortune as a show, and when that was played out, you could easily get up a company to run it as a business concern. You've no monkeys, but, lord, you are rich in sea birds! I can't bring in the birds yet,' he murmured, as another plaintive note of a night watcher sounded from the outside. 'I can't bring in the birds.'

In another instant, he had turned himself off at the main a second time, and was fast asleep.

CHAPTER XXIV.

A PARAGRAPH.

THERE was no sleep for me. This seemed the final stroke of treason against the happiness of sentient life. I had done my best to spoil humanity's share of it, till Victoria entered her *caveat* against the crime; and here was this sleeping figure, as my logical sequel, with all animate Nature for his mark.

It was a distressing thought, and I looked round for something to drive it away. The Captain's bundle of newspapers lay on a chair, and I took them up to read myself to sleep.

I might as well have taken coffee as an opiate. As I turned these fatal leaves, life in all its littleness seemed to beat in upon me, with a suffocating rush, from every quarter of the globe. I was in the fever-struck crowd once more, after my spiritual quarantine of months. It was as a coming back to consciousness after chloroform : my brain throbbed, every pulsation was pain. I darted from column to column, from page to page. I had lost the art of selection : one thing was as another thing, and each impression was a shock. Once again, I realised Europe and America, Asia and Africa, but only as masses in a whirl. The Ball itself, with all its continents, seemed to have suddenly whizzed my way, as I lay dreaming on a cloud in space. Every particle was in movement, as well as the mass; it was a huge rolling cheese, putrid with unwholesome being —a low-bred world, not a world at all, a mere glorified back-court, with all its cheatings, thefts, lies, cruelties, small cares, and small ambitions, multiplied into themselves, and into one another, to make a whole. The finer things alone seemed without an entry, as though, in a business reckoning, such trifles could not count.

I did not know how to read it. Picking and choosing was impossible; I took it as it came. 'Brigandage in the public Thoroughfares ;' 'Foreign Paupers blocking the City Streets ;' 'Outrages on English Fishermen ;'

'Parliament—two Members suspended;' 'Afghanistan—Five hundred killed;' 'Moonlighting in Ireland; a Policeman's Head beaten to Pulp;' 'Evictions—Death of an Old Woman on the Roadside;' 'A Hundred People Burned to Death in a Theatre;' 'Brutal Treatment of a Boy.' This was from the English budget. The American was more appalling in the cool devilry of its mocking headlines, as though all the woe and all the folly of the world were but one stupendous joke—'Green Immigrants sold like Cattle;' 'Awful Railway Accident; the Line stripped bare by Speculators, and no Money to Pay for Repairs;' 'Mr. Chown's Dyspepsia; In the Acquisition of Millions, his Digestion had to go;' 'A Crank writing a weekly Begging-Letter for Fourteen Years, asking for $50,000 to start a Newspaper;' 'No Holiday for Philadelphia's wealthiest Bachelor; Watching his large Interests, and Keeping the Run of Quotations all through the Hot Spell;' 'Mistaken Parsimony makes the Insane Asylum a Pest Hole of Disease;' 'Schevitch voted an Idiot;' 'The last Wrinkle in Thieving;' 'Socialists cry "Rats;"' 'Carbolic Acid isn't Holy Water;'

'The Bulk of the Jewelry melted into Bars;' 'Marvellous Anecdotes of the Altitudinous Aristocracy of Great Britain;' 'Society at Saratoga—another Brilliant Week;' 'Prosperity of the Country; a lady with Thirty-eight Trunks;' 'Pa says he likes Saratoga, because he has a Private Wire to the Stock Exchange.'

And then, suddenly, in one of our own papers, my own name.

'Henry is altogether inaccurate as to the disappearance of poor Lord ——. He has been missing, or, at any rate, away from home, for nearly a year, instead of " for the better part of two months." The family at —— Court have tried to keep the matter out of the newspapers, and that, no doubt, is why Henry has not heard of it till now. Others, who were better informed, kept silent, because they did not wish to cause unnecessary alarm.'

––––––––

'It is certainly true that the shock has been too much for the poor Dowager-Countess, and that her condition causes the gravest

uneasiness. Lord ——— was her favourite son.
It is not true that he has been heard from
only once since he left England. At the outset, he wrote from Paris, as well as from
Genoa.'

———

'The Genoa letter was somewhat enig-
matical:—"Running away for a ramble; news
when I come back." This naturally excited
the Dowager's apprehensions. The police
were consulted, somewhat too soon, and they
discovered that he had been seen at Geneva in
rather questionable company. The Dowager
immediately jumped to the conclusion that he
had fallen into a Nihilist snare. From that
moment, she refused to believe that he was
alive, and, though a subsequent letter bearing
his signature was shown to her, she declined
to accept the evidence of his handwriting.'

———

'Henry is doubly wrong in saying that
Lord ——— was never heard of after the Genoa
letter. A few weeks ago, direct news of him
was received in a rather extraordinary way.
During her late cruise in the South Seas,
H.M.S. "Rollo" touched at one of the Islands

(I forget which), and there, in the best of health and spirits, she found the missing man. He had fallen under the spell of a native beauty, and, I believe, was about to get himself tattooed, as a preliminary to adoption by the tribe. He sent affectionate messages to his family, but he could not be prevailed upon to make any promise of an immediate return.'

'The messages have been communicated to the Dowager, but she persists in regarding them with incredulity. She is persuaded that Lord —— fell a victim to foul play at Genoa, or Geneva, and that all these communications have been forged in his name. Her delusions constitute the only serious feature of the case. These are the facts, if Henry will condescend to accept them as such for the benefit of his readers ; and I may further inform him that —— Court has been shut up.'

CHAPTER XXV.

ANOTHER PARTING.

I DROPPED the paper, and lay staring at the wall, with aching eyeballs, till long past dawn. What my thoughts were, need not be told. They were hardly thoughts ; they were only pangs of remorse.

Then, suddenly, I rose, dressed in all haste, saved my paper from the leafy litter of the night, and went out to find the girl.

I met her, almost on the threshold, fresh from her morning dip in the sea ; and, without greeting, put the paper in her hand— ' Victoria, what must I do ? '

I watched her face as she read, and saw all its glow of youth and health die suddenly to an ashen cast. There was something so awful in the change that, without another word, I walked away.

When I returned to the house, the Ancient

and the Skipper were alone, with the remains of their breakfast before them. Victoria, to all appearance, had served the meal as conscientiously as though nothing had happened. The old man pressed me to eat, and I broke bread.

'No one seems to have any appetite this morning but you and me, Captain,' he said. 'I wonder what's the matter with my girl?'

There was dead silence. I would not answer, and the Captain could not. He seemed to have an instinctive aversion to situations of that sort, and he began to resume the conversation which my entrance had interrupted.

'Yes, sir, off to-morrow morning; repairs or no repairs. Time's up. I've betted a hat on this voyage. It's a go-as-you-please match against time, for the circumnavigation of the globe. Don't try to keep me; I shall lose my hat!'

Victoria entered. If the red had not come back to her cheek, the sickening white had left. She seemed quite calm.

'Our guest is going away to-morrow, girl,

said the old man. ‘Tell him how we hate to say good-bye.’

‘Both our guests are going away, my father,’ was Victoria’s reply.

Her stern serenity seemed to preclude debate. I could only look at her. The old man, speechless, too, for the moment, glanced from one to the other of us. Even the Captain seemed roused to a perception of something out of the common.

‘Both going away,’ repeated the Ancient, after a pause. ‘Surely you, sir——’

‘My father,’ said Victoria gently, ‘I know what I am saying ; and our friend knows it too. He must go. Let us try to thank God that we have kept him so long.’

‘What’s amiss?’ inquired the old man. ‘What have we done? I’ve always wanted him to think that he is master here.’

‘Dearest friend !’ I said, taking his honest hand—I could say no more.

‘This is it, my father,’ said the girl, coming to where we sat, and kissing the old man. ‘Our friend’s life is not our life. He has his own people, and his people call him. They have been calling to him ever since he came to us, and last night their voice reached him half way round the world. The time has come for another parting, that is all. Sooner or later, all things end that way with us. Our little Island is the house of parting, and God has made us to live alone.'

'If I only knew what we had done amiss!' repeated the foolish old man.

'Oh, father, won't you try to understand?' she said, kissing him tenderly, again. 'See what is written here,' and she gave him the paper. 'But you cannot know all it means. I will tell you, if only our friends will leave us together for a little while.'

We went out. The Captain, feeling the situation beyond him, had fallen into a watchful silence. I satisfied his natural curiosity in a few words, as soon as we were outside. I was glad of that relief of speech, such as it was. There was no relief possible, in utterance, for my deeper thoughts. I wanted something to rouse me from what seemed a creeping torpor of death.

It came, as we made our way through the settlement. The child that had been the herald of my coming was now the herald of my going. She was Victoria's favourite, and she had perhaps received a hint when the girl's resolution was formed. At any rate, the sprite was running from house to house, as briskly as on the day of that first message :—'Mother, mother! here's a lord.' It was that scene again with a difference—the people trooping out of their cottages, the women crying, the men pressing forward to wring my hand, and all asking questions at once in the third person, though they seemed to be addressed to me; 'Why is he going? What has happened? How did he get the message? Oh, his poor mother! Will she ever forgive us? Thirteen thousand miles away! Make him promise to come back. What will Victoria do?' As they talked, others could be seen running towards us from the distant fields, leaving their work as they got wind of the dire report. 'Business was suspended' for the day.

Then the Ancient left his house, and joined the group. He held up his hand, and they gathered about him in full plebiscitary meeting of the settlement. 'Friends,' he said, 'we are going to lose a brother. I hoped to keep him for ever, but Victoria says he must go. I hoped he would forget the way back, and the home he left behind ; but something has come to remind him of it. Even now I do not well know what it is, but something has come. The women, I think, will understand it better than we do. I hoped he would stay with us, and be our guide and teacher, and let me take my rest. We want a helper to show us how they do things out in the great world. Some say we are happier without it—who can tell? We are as children that have never known a mother's knee. He could have shown us the way. I must not ask him to stay : Victoria says he ought to go, and Victoria knows' (voices, ' Yes, Victoria knows'). 'If I might ask him, I would say, "Take all you want here—all it is in our power to give—my place, my bit of land——"'

' Give him the long field under the Ridge!' cried the voices again ; ' Build a house for him ! Make him magistrate next year ! Have two magistrates ! '

All turned towards me. I shook my head. The children clustered about me, cry- ing, and soon, with their treble, was mingled a deeper note of woe. How shall words paint the misery of that scene? As I had felt before, so I felt now—a rage of pity for the sorrow that seems to be our lot in life.

A word or act of power and control was wanting; and it came. Victoria, tearless, and with the set look on her face that I had caught for an instant on the day she saved my life at the Cave, stepped into our midst, and drew the old man aside. After that, not a word was spoken, and the assembly seemed to melt away.

Victoria had become the leader of the settlement; no one seemed to question her commands. They were not commands so much as imperious wishes which all divined. It was understood that the Captain was to give me passage to Europe; he was never asked to do it. Still less, was I asked if I would take the passage. Victoria pushed forward my departure with an energy, controlling and controlled, worthy of a crisis of battle. She stood on the beach while the whale boat laboured to and fro betwixt ship and shore to complete our exchange of stores with the American. The presents of the Islanders to

me made the better part of an entire load.
I had brought nothing to the Island but the
clothes in which I stood upright, and a roll of
paper money which the Ancient had always
refused to diminish by the substance of a
single note. The money had not been useless,
for all that. It had enabled me to make
some purchases, to repair my outfit, on the
coming of the Queen's ship, and now it pro-
cured from the crew of the trader a few
presents for my generous hosts.

The excitement of these preparations
helped to suspend the anguish of parting.
But, at nightfall, this returned with cruel
force, when the people gathered on the moonlit
green, to sing me their simple songs of farewell. It was the whole settlement, save one:
Victoria was not to be found. They came with
cheerful faces: the sorrow of the morning,
I knew, would be renewed in due season, but
their natures lived ever in the moment as it
passed. The children prattled and played;
and, in the murmur of talk among their elders,
there was no note of woe. Under the shining
sun, it might have been a scene of joy; and,
if the moonlight touched it into sadness, this

was but a spiritual association of ideas. They sang all that they thought would please me, all that I had ever liked—the joyous songs, of course, in preference. All were sad songs to me. At last, with slow and measured cadence, their perfect voices rising in the perfect night, they began the one I had always loved most. It was a song of parting and of death, with the burden, ' When I am gone—when I am gone.'

Before the second stanza was over, I had stolen from my place in the shadow, with such a passion of sorrow stirring to the very depths of my being, as I had never known in all my life.

CHAPTER XXVI.

AN EXPLANATION.

I walked away in unutterable despondency, relieved only by one purpose, one hope—to find Victoria. I had not far to go to seek her: her statuesque form was outlined against the clear sky above the Peak.

She turned to greet me with a grave smile.

'You came away before it was over; I was wiser than you, I came away before it began. I suppose it is because we are wild people that we make such a ceremony of saying "Good-bye." Before they taught us to be Christians, you know, we used to make just the same fuss about death.'

'Is it good-bye, Victoria? I hardly know what it is. It looks like dismissal, without a word of leave-taking. You seem to have sent me away.'

'I *have* sent you away,' she said, her

voice trembling a little, and then instantly recovering its tone. ‘ Yes, I want always to be able to feel that I told you, when the time had come, to go.’

A pang shot through my heart that was not regret, but a sort of jealous rage.

‘ You are a great observer of times and seasons, Victoria. Perhaps, even now, I have lingered too long.’

‘ Perhaps,’ she said, with the note deeper, richer than before, but no less firm. Then she added, as though to make her meaning more clear :

‘ If there were all the reasons in the world for keeping you, dearest friend, you must still go, to save your mother’s life. You feel the force of that reason as much as I do. Why seek for more ? ’

‘ That reason, from myself to myself, Victoria, may be enough. It is not enough from you to me.’

‘ From me to you then,’ she said ; ‘ will this do ? All things leave us, as we stand here in this Isle ; all things pass us by. Whatever comes to us, as surely goes. Why should we hope to keep it, when that must be the end ?

God has marked us out for solitude : let us bow to God's will. Nothing could keep you here : it is written. Nothing has kept others.'

The pang that had almost ceased darted through me again with its full force, at these last words. 'Cold, cruel heart !' I said in a fury of pain, ' you have never cared to keep me. Why had you not pity enough to let me die, when the waves tossed me here ? '

She gave me one glance, of which I could not catch the full expression in the uncertain light, straightened herself, folded her hands behind her, and turned her face towards the sea.

The wrathful agony of my feelings endured even under this rebuke, much as I felt I deserved it. I was distinctly aware that I was playing a pitiful part before her, and distinctly unable to help playing it. The torment of losing her, of being nothing to her, overpowered every finer feeling : and the more I felt the degradation of my violence, the more desperate the violence seemed to become. I felt only the goading of the pain of loss, and, forgetting all my fine resolves to treat her with the disdain with which I thought she was treating me, I caught her in my arms and covered her lips, her eyes, her brow, with passionate kisses, till she sank for support upon a jutting stone. It was no timid first kiss of pastoral flirtation, but twenty, following as quick on one another as a rain of angry blows. There was a sort of anger in them, as well as love. I seemed to feel that I had been made the sport of her innocence. What had I not lost by trying to outdo her in tenderness, in generosity, and reserve? So I interpret my feelings now: at the moment, nothing could have been more devoid of conscious motive than the madness of this act. The brute that is in each of us, and that is only half held in check by laws, observances, and uses, seemed suddenly to have slipped his chain.

Yet, if the act was a surprise to me, in itself, it was a greater surprise in its effect upon Victoria. The girl seemed to sink down, from sheer want of the power of resistance. The lips parted, without word or sound, but the eyes met the fierce gaze of mine with infinite tenderness; and, when she did speak, this was what I heard:

'Oh, I love you, I love you—better than

my own life : and I will never have you love me : and to-morrow you shall go away from me for ever.'

The thing had been said, and there was no unsaying it. In vain, Victoria, resuming her self-control almost as quickly as she had lost it, disengaged herself from my arms, which had sought her beautiful shape.

She sat silent, in what I could not but feel was a silence of shame. For the moment, I was silent too. We were both, in a manner, stunned by the shock of that avowal. Victoria had said what she meant never to say : I had heard what I never hoped to hear. If I had expectation of anything—though, indeed, I think I had none—it was rather of anger and fierce repulse.

I was the first to recover speech, if not self-possession. I took her hand : thank Heaven I had enough sense and feeling left not to claim her lips on the strength of what had just passed. I tried to tell her something of what I had wanted to tell her all this weary time—how my love for her had come, first, through the divine suggestion of her shape, and voice, and ways, and how her soul had completed what they had begun, and turned enchantment into one of the laws of being.

She listened, and soon, as I could see, no longer with shame. The hand I held returned the pressure of my own, and I felt the thrilling touch of the other on my brow and hair.

She spoke at last. 'Listen, dear friend: now all must be said. It is too late to blame you for what has happened, or even to blame myself for letting it happen. It was to be. No human soul could be angry that knew how I tried, not even——'

I would not let her utter the name. 'Never speak of him. What can he be to you? What fate does he deserve?' but she laid her finger on my lips.

'I know; my heart is yours, but only he shall release my hand.'

'Victoria!'

'Oh! listen, listen, and be still! I know all that must be said, and all that must be done.

'When you first came, my heart was his, or I thought it was. I thought it had gone out with him into the world—your world, or the next one, they are both just as far away from us. I don't know what I felt about you, except that I felt what was good and true and right. Was it wrong to like you? How can anyone help liking you that knows you? You spoke to me as no one had spoken to me before. You seemed to know all things. I only wanted to listen to you, and still be true to him. All my hope of myself was in being true. Our people do not always know what that sort of truth is. There are the two strains in our blood; we are English, and something else. It has shocked me, from my girlhood up, to see how we sometimes forget. We feel so quickly; and all our feeling is in each terrible moment as it flies. I set myself above our people; I shuddered to think I should ever be like that. My love was part of my respect for myself. Half our women have had their love tokens taken away in Queen's ships, and have still lived on to be wives and mothers in the Isle. I could not, I would not be like that.

'I did not blame then; I pitied! It is all so splendid when the Queen's ships come. The young men in them seem to have dropped from the sky. It is like the book of the Heathen mythology, with the gods coming down.

' When I saw you, I did not know it was to be like that. I felt sure of myself, and, if I had doubted, still I should have felt sure of you. Then slowly, slowly, slowly, came the dreadful change, though, if you had not spoken that day, I might never have known that it had come. When I did know, still it did not seem to be too late. My pride was strong: I did not know the strength of my weakness. I went there every day—to the thicket, and prayed to have him sent back to me. I tried to shut you quite out from my heart, but still to keep you in my soul. You were so good; you made me think I had done it. You tried to make me think so; I knew you tried; and your very goodness only made it worse and worse.

' Then, I felt I was no longer sure of myself. I tried to keep away from you; but, to have you near me, and not to see you, not to speak to you, made all the world seem dead and cold. So, I always came back to find you again, of my own accord, wanting to keep all my happiness, when I ought to have chosen which part of it I should give up.'

'Victoria, if only I had known; if only I had understood!'

'Oh, how dreadful, if you thought me light-minded, playing you off and on. All that I wanted was to like you as much as I dared, without having you like me more than you ought. I should have done, what I see now I must do—send you away, for both our sakes. If I did not see it at once, pity, dear friend, pity, and forgive!

'Then, I prayed again for help; and see how the help has come! We might both of us have been too weak for that sacrifice, but now it is laid upon us without our wills. You must go.'

'I will come back, come to claim you, my Victoria, to bring you your word of release, to take you, whether you will or no.'

'You will never come back,' she said in a tone that seemed to be beyond both hope and despair, and she held my face up to the light and looked down into it with tender yet tear-less eyes. 'You ought not to come back: your place is in the great world—poor little great world! Try to think there is something nobler than love for one—pity for all. Go: and live for those poor people you have talked about to me.'

'I am not equal to it: I could only die for them, at best.'

'Still—I know what I am saying—others must claim you: your station——'

'O Victoria, is your opinion of me so low? Do you send me back to resume the "English gentleman"; and to hide my shame in being nothing in the smug proprieties of that poor creature's lot?'

'I do not know, dear friend, but this I feel—we must lose you for ever: no one returns here.'

'Then let me never go away,' I cried, rising, and clasping her again to my heart. 'Let me love you, and be with you for ever, and forget all the world beside.'

Once more I saw a beginning of that exquisite languor which had almost made her mine. The lips of the beautiful creature parted, but only in sighs; the eyes closed. Once more, too, my own lips approached them, when the girl roused herself, by some mysterious exertion of will, tore herself from my embrace, and ran to the very edge of the cliff.

'Deep into the deep sea, beloved one, for ever beloved of my heart, if you come one step more! Go now, go from me, and leave me to say my prayers. I love you ; take that last word from Victoria ; you will never hear her voice again.'

'She shall hear mine. After such a last word, my Victoria, there must be more. If you could have told me I was nothing to you, I would have gone for ever ; now, Death alone shall part you and me. Go, I must, for a season, but your blessed promise, for promise it is, makes it almost easy to say farewell. Be sure of this, I will come back to claim you, from the other side of the world. I will leave you now, since my presence troubles you ; I will even set sail without trying to speak to you again. But, before I go, you *shall* give me a sign or a token—a token of submission, my Victoria, I claim no less, a sign that you have conquered your foolish superstition of fidelity, and your cruel pride.'

CHAPTER XXVII.

THE PROMISE OF THE SKIES.

I HAD no room-fellow that night. The Captain had gone on board, to sleep, leaving word that he would fire his signal-gun very early in the morning. I should have been ready for it, if it had come at dawn.

The day was but just breaking, when I heard someone stirring in the next room. I ran in, with I know not what wild hope, but only to find the old man.

He was standing near the recess that formed her bed-chamber, with the sliding panel in his hand, and staring helplessly at the empty bed. It had not been used that night.

The glance he turned on me was enough; I did not wait for his words, but rushed out of the house.

That horror, thank God, was a false alarm. The child who was her favourite was running towards our cottage with a message that should have been delivered the night before. She had passed the night under a neighbour's roof.

As I hurried back with the news to the old man, I heard the signal gun.

A week has passed, yet I cannot clearly recall what followed. I am dimly aware of a last look at the cottage and the settlement, of a crowd of weeping villagers, of the grasp of the Ancient's hand. There is an almost absolute void of perception between the boat at the landing-stage, and the ship, with her solitary passenger, flying at full speed from the shore. Active consciousness seems to have been suspended between these two decisive facts. Memory is resumed, with one ineffaceable impression that it must hold for life—Victoria stretching her arms towards the ship, from the summit of the Peak. As she stood there, with her background of fleecy cloud, she seemed rather of heaven than of earth, and her gesture was a promise of the skies. Then, I knew that it was well with me; and I turned my face from the Island with a joyful heart.

Spottiswoode & Co. Printers, New-street Square, London.

GENERAL LISTS OF WORKS

PUBLISHED BY

MESSRS. LONGMANS, GREEN, & CO.

39 PATERNOSTER ROW, LONDON, E.C.; AND
15 EAST 16th STREET, NEW YORK.

————∞≻⊙≺∞————

HISTORY, POLITICS, HISTORICAL MEMOIRS, &c.

Abbey's The English Church and its Bishops, 1700–1800. 2 vols. 8vo. 24s.

Abbey and Overton's English Church in the Eighteenth Century. Cr. 8vo. 7s. 6d.

Arnold's Lectures on Modern History. 8vo. 7s. 6d.

Bagwell's Ireland under the Tudors. Vols. 1 and 2. 2 vols. 8vo. 32s.

Ball's The Reformed Church of Ireland, 1537–1886. 8vo. 7s. 6d.

Boultbee's History of the Church of England, Pre-Reformation Period. 8vo. 15s.

Buckle's History of Civilisation. 3 vols. crown 8vo. 24s.

Cox's (Sir G. W.) General History of Greece. Crown 8vo. Maps, 7s. 6d.

Creighton's History of the Papacy during the Reformation. 8vo. Vols. 1 and 2, 32s. Vols. 3 and 4, 24s.

De Tocqueville's Democracy in America. 2 vols. crown 8vo. 16s.

D'Herisson's The Black Cabinet. Crown 8vo. 7s. 6d.

Doyle's English in America : Virginia, Maryland, and the Carolinas, 8vo. 18s.
— — — The Puritan Colonies, 2 vols. 8vo. 36s.

Epochs of Ancient History. Edited by the Rev. Sir G. W. Cox, Bart. and C. Sankey, M.A. With Maps. Fcp. 8vo. price 2s. 6d. each.

Beesly's Gracchi, Marius, and Sulla.	Ihne's Rome to its Capture by the Gauls.
Capes's Age of the Antonines.	Merivale's Roman Triumvirates.
— Early Roman Empire.	Sankey's Spartan and Theban Supremacies.
Cox's Athenian Empire.	
— Greeks and Persians.	
Curteis's Rise of the Macedonian Empire.	Smith's Rome and Carthage, the Punic Wars.

Epochs of Modern History. Edited by C. Colbeck, M.A. With Maps. Fcp. 8vo. price 2s. 6d. each.

Church's Beginning of the Middle Ages.	Longman's Frederick the Great and the Seven Years' War.
Cox's Crusades.	Ludlow's War of American Independence.
Creighton's Age of Elizabeth.	
Gairdner's Houses of Lancaster and York.	M'Carthy's Epoch of Reform, 1830–1850.
Gardiner's Puritan Revolution.	Moberly's The Early Tudors.
— Thirty Years' War.	Morris's Age of Queen Anne.
— (Mrs.) French Revolution, 1789–1795.	— The Early Hanoverians.
	Seebohm's Protestant Revolution.
Hale's Fall of the Stuarts.	Stubbs's The Early Plantagenets.
Johnson's Normans in Europe.	Warburton's Edward III.

Epochs of Church History. Edited by the Rev. Mandell Creighton, M.A. Fcp. 8vo. price 2s. 6d. each.

Brodrick's A History of the University of Oxford.	Perry's The Reformation in England.
Carr's The Church and the Roman Empire.	Plummer's The Church of the Early Fathers.
Overton's The Evangelical Revival in the Eighteenth Century.	Tucker's The English Church in other Lands.

₊ *Other Volumes in preparation.*

LONGMANS, GREEN, & CO. London and New York.

Freeman's Historical Geography of Europe. 2 vols. 8vo. 31*s*. 6*d*.

Froude's English in Ireland in the 18th Century. 3 vols. crown 8vo. 18*s*.

— History of England. Popular Edition. 12 vols. crown 8vo. 3*s*. 6*d*. each.

Gardiner's History of England from the Accession of James I. to the Outbreak of the Civil War. 10 vols. crown 8vo. 60*s*.

— History of the Great Civil War, 1642–1649 (3 vols.) Vol. 1, 1642–1644, 8vo. 21*s*.

Greville's Journal of the Reign of Queen Victoria, 1837–1852. 3 vols. 8vo. 36*s*. 1852–1860, 2 vols. 8vo. 24*s*.

Historic Towns. Edited by E. A. Freeman, D.C.L. and the Rev. William Hunt, M.A. With Maps and Plans. Crown 8vo. 3*s*. 6*d*. each.

London. By W. E. Loftie.	Bristol. By the Rev. W. Hunt.
Exeter. By E. A. Freeman.	Oxford. By the Rev. C. W. Boase.

    *** Other volumes in preparation.*

Lecky's History of England in the Eighteenth Century. Vols. 1 & 2, 1700–1760, 8vo. 36*s*. Vols. 3 & 4, 1760–1784, 8vo. 36*s*. Vols. 5 & 6, 1784–1793, 36*s*.

— History of European Morals. 2 vols. crown 8vo. 16*s*.

— — — Rationalism in Europe. 2 vols. crown 8vo. 16*s*.

Longman's Life and Times of Edward III. 2 vols. 8vo. 28*s*.

Macaulay's Complete Works. Library Edition. 8 vols. 8vo. £5. 5*s*.

— — — Cabinet Edition. 16 vols. crown 8vo. £4. 16*s*.

— History of England :—

Student's Edition. 2 vols. cr. 8vo. 12*s*.	Cabinet Edition. 8 vols. post 8vo. 48*s*.
People's Edition. 4 vols. cr. 8vo. 16*s*.	Library Edition. 5 vols. 8vo. £4.

Macaulay's Critical and Historical Essays, with Lays of Ancient Rome In One Volume :—

Authorised Edition. Cr. 8vo. 2*s*. 6*d*. or 3*s*. 6*d*. gilt edges.	Popular Edition. Cr. 8vo. 2*s*. 6*d*.

Macaulay's Critical and Historical Essays :—

Student's Edition. 1 vol. cr. 8vo. 6*s*.	Cabinet Edition. 4 vols. post 8vo. 24*s*.
People's Edition. 2 vols. cr. 8vo. 8*s*.	Library Edition. 3 vols. 8vo. 36*s*.

Macaulay's Speeches corrected by Himself. Crown 8vo. 3*s*. 6*d*.

Malmesbury's (Earl of) Memoirs of an Ex-Minister. Crown 8vo. 7*s*. 6*d*.

May's Constitutional History of England, 1760–1870. 3 vols. crown 8vo. 18*s*.

— Democracy in Europe. 2 vols. 8vo. 32*s*.

Merivale's Fall of the Roman Republic. 12mo. 7*s*. 6*d*.

— General History of Rome, B.C. 753–A.D. 476. Crown 8vo. 7*s*. 6*d*.

— History of the Romans under the Empire. 8 vols. post 8vo. 48*s*.

Nelson's (Lord) Letters and Despatches. Edited by J. K. Laughton. 8vo. 16*s*.

Pears' The Fall of Constantinople. 8vo. 16*s*.

Saintsbury's Manchester : a Short History. Crown 8vo. 3*s*. 6*d*.

Seebohm's Oxford Reformers—Colet, Erasmus, & More. 8vo. 14*s*.

Short's History of the Church of England. Crown 8vo. 7*s*. 6*d*.

Smith's Carthage and the Carthaginians. Crown 8vo. 10*s*. 6*d*.

Taylor's Manual of the History of India. Crown 8vo. 7*s*. 6*d*.

Todd's Parliamentary Government in England (2 vols.) Vol. 1, 8vo. 21*s*.

Vitzthum's St. Petersburg and London, 1852–1864. 2 vols. 8vo. 30*s*.

Walpole's History of England, from 1815. 5 vols. 8vo. Vols. 1 & 2, 1815–1832, 36*s*. Vol. 3, 1832–1841, 18*s*. Vols. 4 & 5, 1841–1858, 36*s*.

Wylie's History of England under Henry IV. Vol. 1, crown 8vo. 10*s*. 6*d*.

LONGMANS, GREEN, & CO., London and New York.

BIOGRAPHICAL WORKS

Armstrong's (E. J.) Life and Letters. Edited by G. F. Armstrong. Fcp. 8vo. 7s.6d.
Bacon's Life and Letters, by Spedding. 7 vols. 8vo. £4. 4s.
Bagehot's Biographical Studies. 1 vol. 8vo. 12s.
Carlyle's Life, by J. A. Froude. Vols. 1 & 2, 1795-1835, 8vo. 32s. Vols. 3 & 4, 1834-1881, 8vo. 32s.
— (Mrs.) Letters and Memorials. 3 vols. 8vo. 36s.
Doyle (Sir F. H.) Reminiscences and Opinions. 8vo. 16s.
English Worthies. Edited by Andrew Lang. Crown 8vo. 2s. 6d. each.

Charles Darwin. By Grant Allen.	Steele. By Austin Dobson.
Shaftesbury (The First Earl). By H. D. Traill.	Ben Jonson. By J. A. Symonds.
	George Canning. By Frank H. Hill.
Admiral Blake. By David Hannay.	Claverhouse. By Mowbray Morris.
Marlborough. By Geo. Saintsbury.	

*** *Other Volumes in preparation.*
Fox (Charles James) The Early History of. By Sir G. O. Trevelyan, Bart. Crown 8vo. 6s.
Froude's Cæsar: a Sketch. Crown 8vo. 6s.
Hamilton's (Sir W. R.) Life, by Graves. Vols. 1 and 2, 8vo. 15s. each.
Havelock's Life, by Marshman. Crown 8vo. 3s. 6d.
Hobart Pacha's Sketches from my Life. Crown 8vo. 7s. 6d.
Macaulay's (Lord) Life and Letters. By his Nephew, Sir G. O. Trevelyan, Bart. Popular Edition, 1 vol. crown 8vo. 6s. Cabinet Edition, 2 vols. post 8vo. 12s. Library Edition, 2 vols. 8vo. 36s.
Mendelssohn's Letters. Translated by Lady Wallace. 2 vols. cr. 8vo. 5s. each.
Mill (James) Biography of, by Prof. Bain. Crown 8vo. 5s.
— (John Stuart) Recollections of, by Prof. Bain. Crown 8vo. 2s. 6d.
— — Autobiography. 8vo. 7s. 6d.
Müller's (Max) Biographical Essays. Crown 8vo. 7s. 6d.
Newman's Apologia pro Vitâ Suâ. Crown 8vo. 6s.
Pasteur (Louis) His Life and Labours. Crown 8vo. 7s. 6d.
Shakespeare's Life (Outlines of), by Halliwell-Phillipps. 2 vols. royal 8vo. 10s. 6d.
Southey's Correspondence with Caroline Bowles. 8vo. 14s.
Stephen's Essays in Ecclesiastical Biography. Crown 8vo. 7s. 6d.
Wellington's Life, by Gleig. Crown 8vo. 6s.

MENTAL AND POLITICAL PHILOSOPHY, FINANCE, &c.

Amos's View of the Science of Jurisprudence. 8vo. 18s.
— Primer of the English Constitution. Crown 8vo. 6s.
Bacon's Essays, with Annotations by Whately. 8vo. 10s. 6d.
— Works, edited by Spedding. 7 vols. 8vo. 73s. 6d.
Bagehot's Economic Studies, edited by Hutton. 8vo. 10s. 6d.
— The Postulates of English Political Economy. Crown 8vo. 2s. 6d.
Bain's Logic, Deductive and Inductive. Crown 8vo. 10s. 6d.
PART I. Deduction, 4s. | PART II. Induction, 6s. 6d.
— Mental and Moral Science. Crown 8vo. 10s. 6d.
— The Senses and the Intellect. 8vo. 15s.
— The Emotions and the Will. 8vo. 15s.
— Practical Essays. Crown 8vo. 4s. 6d.

LONGMANS, GREEN, & CO., London and New York.

Buckle's (H. T.) Miscellaneous and Posthumous Works. 2 vols. crown 8vo. 21s.
Crump's A Short Enquiry into the Formation of English Political Opinion. 8vo. 7s. 6d.
Dowell's A History of Taxation and Taxes in England. 4 vols. 8vo. 48s.
Green's (Thomas Hill) Works. (3 vols.) Vols. 1 & 2, Philosophical Works. 8vo. 16s. each.
Hume's Essays, edited by Green & Grose. 2 vols. 8vo. 28s.
    — Treatise of Human Nature, edited by Green & Grose. 2 vols. 8vo. 28s.
Ladd's Elements of Physiological Psychology. 8vo. 21s.
Lang's Custom and Myth : Studies of Early Usage and Belief. Crown 8vo. 7s. 6d.
Leslie's Essays in Political and Moral Philosophy. 8vo. 10s. 6d.
Lewes's History of Philosophy. 2 vols. 8vo. 32s.
Lubbock's Origin of Civilisation. 8vo. 18s.
Macleod's Principles of Economical Philosophy. In 2 vols. Vol. 1, 8vo. 15s. Vol. 2, Part I. 12s.
    — The Elements of Economics. (2 vols.) Vol. 1, cr. 8vo. 7s. 6d. Vol. 2, Part I. cr. 8vo. 7s. 6d.
    — The Elements of Banking. Crown 8vo. 5s.
    — The Theory and Practice of Banking. Vol. 1, 8vo. 12s. Vol. 2, 14s.
    — Economics for Beginners. 8vo. 2s. 6d.
    — Lectures on Credit and Banking. 8vo. 5s.
Mill's (James) Analysis of the Phenomena of the Human Mind. 2 vols. 8vo. 28s.
Mill (John Stuart) on Representative Government. Crown 8vo. 2s.
    —   —   on Liberty. Crown 8vo. 1s. 4d.
    —   —   Examination of Hamilton's Philosophy. 8vo. 16s.
    —   —   Logic. Crown 8vo. 5s.
    —   —   Principles of Political Economy. 2 vols. 8vo. 30s. People's Edition, 1 vol. crown 8vo. 5s.
    —   —   Subjection of Women. Crown 8vo. 6s.
    —   —   Utilitarianism. 8vo. 5s.
    —   —   Three Essays on Religion, &c. 8vo. 5s.
Mulhall's History of Prices since 1850. Crown 8vo. 6s.
Müller's The Science of Thought. 8vo. 21s.
Sandars's Institutes of Justinian, with English Notes. 8vo. 18s.
Seebohm's English Village Community. 8vo. 16s.
Sully's Outlines of Psychology. 8vo. 12s. 6d.
    — Teacher's Handbook of Psychology. Crown 8vo. 6s. 6d.
Swinburne's Picture Logic. Post 8vo. 5s.
Thompson's A System of Psychology. 2 vols. 8vo. 36s.
    — The Problem of Evil. 8vo. 10s. 6d.
Thomson's Outline of Necessary Laws of Thought. Crown 8vo. 6s.
Twiss's Law of Nations in Time of War. 8vo. 21s.
    —   —   in Time of Peace. 8vo. 15s.
Webb's The Veil of Isis. 8vo. 10s. 6d.
Whately's Elements of Logic. Crown 8vo. 4s. 6d.
    —   — Rhetoric. Crown 8vo. 4s. 6d.
Wylie's Labour, Leisure, and Luxury. Crown 8vo. 6s.
Zeller's History of Eclecticism in Greek Philosophy. Crown 8vo. 10s. 6d.
    — Plato and the Older Academy. Crown 8vo. 18s.
    — Pre-Socratic Schools. 2 vols. crown 8vo. 30s.
    — Socrates and the Socratic Schools. Crown 8vo. 10s. 6d.
    — Stoics, Epicureans, and Sceptics. Crown 8vo. 15s.
    — Outlines of the History of Greek Philosophy. Crown 8vo. 10s. 6d.

LONGMANS, GREEN, & CO., London and New York.

MISCELLANEOUS WORKS.

A. K. H. B., The Essays and Contributions of. Crown 8vo.

    Autumn Holidays of a Country Parson. 3s. 6d.

    Changed Aspects of Unchanged Truths. 3s. 6d.

    Common-Place Philosopher in Town and Country. 3s. 6d.

    Critical Essays of a Country Parson. 3s. 6d.

    Counsel and Comfort spoken from a City Pulpit. 3s. 6d.

    Graver Thoughts of a Country Parson. Three Series. 3s. 6d. each.

    Landscapes, Churches, and Moralities. 3s. 6d.

    Leisure Hours in Town. 3s. 6d. Lessons of Middle Age. 3s. 6d.

    Our Homely Comedy; and Tragedy. 3s. 6d.

    Our Little Life. Essays Consolatory and Domestic. Two Series. 3s. 6d.

    Present-day Thoughts. 3s. 6d.   [each.

    Recreations of a Country Parson. Three Series. 3s. 6d. each.

    Seaside Musings on Sundays and Week-Days. 3s. 6d.

    Sunday Afternoons in the Parish Church of a University City. 3s. 6d.

Armstrong's (Ed. J.) Essays and Sketches. Fcp. 8vo. 5s.

Arnold's (Dr. Thomas) Miscellaneous Works. 8vo. 7s. 6d.

Bagehot's Literary Studies, edited by Hutton. 2 vols. 8vo. 28s.

Beaconsfield (Lord), The Wit and Wisdom of. Crown 8vo. 1s. boards; 1s. 6d. cl.

Evans's Bronze Implements of Great Britain. 8vo. 25s.

Farrar's Language and Languages. Crown 8vo. 6s.

Froude's Short Studies on Great Subjects. 4 vols. crown 8vo. 24s.

Lang's Letters to Dead Authors. Fcp. 8vo. 6s. 6d.

  — Books and Bookmen. Crown 8vo. 6s. 6d.

Macaulay's Miscellaneous Writings. 2 vols. 8vo. 21s. 1 vol. crown 8vo. 4s. 6d.

  — Miscellaneous Writings and Speeches. Crown 8vo. 6s.

  — Miscellaneous Writings, Speeches, Lays of Ancient Rome, &c. Cabinet Edition. 4 vols. crown 8vo. 24s.

  — Writings, Selections from. Crown 8vo. 6s.

Müller's (Max) Lectures on the Science of Language. 2 vols. crown 8vo. 16s.

  — — Lectures on India. 8vo. 12s. 6d.

Proctor's Chance and Luck. Crown 8vo. 5s.

Smith (Sydney) The Wit and Wisdom of. Crown 8vo. 1s. boards; 1s. 6d. cloth.

ASTRONOMY.

Herschel's Outlines of Astronomy. Square crown 8vo. 12s.

Proctor's Larger Star Atlas. Folio, 15s. or Maps only, 12s. 6d.

  — New Star Atlas. Crown 8vo. 5s.

  — Light Science for Leisure Hours. 3 Series. Crown 8vo. 5s. each.

  — The Moon. Crown 8vo. 6s.

  — Other Worlds than Ours. Crown 8vo. 5s.

  — The Sun. Crown 8vo. 14s.

  — Studies of Venus-Transits. 8vo. 5s.

  — Orbs Around Us. Crown 8vo. 5s.

  — Universe of Stars. 8vo. 10s. 6d.

Webb's Celestial Objects for Common Telescopes. Crown 8vo. 9s.

THE 'KNOWLEDGE' LIBRARY.
Edited by RICHARD A. PROCTOR.

How to Play Whist. Crown 8vo. 5s.

Home Whist. 16mo. 1s.

The Borderland of Science. Cr. 8vo. 6s.

Nature Studies. Crown 8vo. 6s.

Leisure Readings. Crown 8vo. 6s.

The Stars in their Seasons. Imp. 8vo. 5s.

Myths and Marvels of Astronomy. Crown 8vo. 6s.

Pleasant Ways in Science. Cr. 8vo. 6s.

Star Primer. Crown 4to. 2s. 6d.

The Seasons Pictured. Demy 4to. 5s.

Strength and Happiness. Cr. 8vo. 5s.

Rough Ways made Smooth. Cr. 8vo. 6s.

The Expanse of Heaven. Cr. 8vo. 5s.

Our Place among Infinities. Cr. 8vo. 5s.

LONGMANS, GREEN, & CO., London and New York.

CLASSICAL LANGUAGES AND LITERATURE.

Æschylus, The Eumenides of. Text, with Metrical English Translation, by J. F. Davies. 8vo. 7*s*.

Aristophanes' The Acharnians, translated by R. Y. Tyrrell. Crown 8vo. 2*s*. 6*d*.

Aristotle's The Ethics, Text and Notes, by Sir Alex. Grant, Bart. 2 vols. 8vo. 32*s*.

— The Nicomachean Ethics, translated by Williams, crown 8vo. 7*s*. 6*d*.

— The Politics, Books I. III. IV. (VII.) with Translation, &c. by Bolland and Lang. Crown 8vo. 7*s*. 6*d*.

Becker's *Charicles* and *Gallus*, by Metcalfe. Post 8vo. 7*s*. 6*d*. each.

Cicero's Correspondence, Text and Notes, by R. Y. Tyrrell. Vols. 1 & 2, 8vo. 12*s*. each.

Homer's Iliad, Homometrically translated by Cayley. 8vo. 12*s*. 6*d*.

— — Greek Text, with Verse Translation, by W. C. Green. Vol. 1, Books I.–XII. Crown 8vo. 6*s*.

Mahaffy's Classical Greek Literature. Crown 8vo. Vol. 1, The Poets, 7*s*. 6*d*. Vol. 2, The Prose Writers, 7*s*. 6*d*.

Plato's Parmenides, with Notes, &c. by J. Maguire. 8vo. 7*s*. 6*d*.

Virgil's Works, Latin Text, with Commentary, by Kennedy. Crown 8vo. 10*s*. 6*d*.

— Æneid, translated into English Verse, by Conington. Crown 8vo. 9*s*.

— — — — — — by W. J. Thornhill. Cr. 8vo. 7*s*.6*d*.

— Poems, — — — Prose, by Conington. Crown 8vo. 9*s*.

Witt's Myths of Hellas, translated by F. M. Younghusband. Crown 8vo. 3*s*. 6*d*.

— The Trojan War, — — Fcp. 8vo. 2*s*.

— The Wanderings of Ulysses, — Crown 8vo. 3*s*. 6*d*.

NATURAL HISTORY, BOTANY, & GARDENING.

Allen's Flowers and their Pedigrees. Crown 8vo. Woodcuts, 5*s*.

Decaisne and Le Maout's General System of Botany. Imperial 8vo. 31*s*. 6*d*.

Dixon's Rural Bird Life. Crown 8vo. Illustrations, 5*s*.

Hartwig's Aerial World, 8vo. 10*s*. 6*d*.

— Polar World, 8vo. 10*s*. 6*d*.

— Sea and its Living Wonders. 8vo. 10*s*. 6*d*.

— Subterranean World, 8vo. 10*s*. 6*d*.

— Tropical World, 8vo. 10*s*. 6*d*.

Lindley's Treasury of Botany. 2 vols. fcp. 8vo. 12*s*.

Loudon's Encyclopædia of Gardening. 8vo. 21*s*.

— — Plants. 8vo. 42*s*.

Rivers's Orchard House. Crown 8vo. 5*s*.

— Miniature Fruit Garden. Fcp. 8vo. 4*s*.

Stanley's Familiar History of British Birds. Crown 8vo. 6*s*.

Wood's Bible Animals. With 112 Vignettes. 8vo. 10*s*. 6*d*.

— Common British Insects. Crown 8vo. 3*s*. 6*d*.

— Homes Without Hands, 8vo. 10*s*. 6*d*.

— Insects Abroad, 8vo. 10*s*. 6*d*.

— Horse and Man. 8vo. 14*s*.

— Insects at Home. With 700 Illustrations. 8vo. 10*s*. 6*d*.

— Out of Doors. Crown 8vo. 5*s*.

— Petland Revisited. Crown 8vo. 7*s*. 6*d*.

— Strange Dwellings. Crown 8vo. 5*s*. Popular Edition, 4to. 6*d*.

LONGMANS, GREEN, & CO., London and New York.

PRIZE AND PRESENTATION BOOKS.

Jameson's Sacred and Legendary Art. 6 vols. square 8vo.

Legends of the Madonna. 1 vol. 21*s*.

— — — Monastic Orders 1 vol. 21*s*.

— — — Saints and Martyrs. 2 vols. 31*s*. 6*d*.

— — — Saviour. Completed by Lady Eastlake. 2 vols. 42*s*.

Macaulay's Lays of Ancient Rome. illustrated by Scharf. Fcp. 4to. 10*s*. 6*d*.

The same, with *Ivry* and the *Armada*, illustrated by Weguelin. Crown 8vo. 3*s*. 6*d*.

New Testament (The) illustrated with Woodcuts after Paintings by the Early Masters. 4to. 21*s*.

By Dr. G. Hartwig.

Sea Monsters and Sea Birds (from 'The Sea and its Living Wonders'). With 75 Illustrations. Crown 8vo. 2*s*. 6*d*. cloth extra, gilt edges.

Denizens of the Deep (from 'The Sea and its Living Wonders'). With 117 Illustrations. Crown 8vo. 2*s*. 6*d*. cloth extra, gilt edges.

Dwellers in the Arctic Regions (from 'The Sea and its Living Wonders'). With 29 Illustrations. Crown 8vo. 2*s*. 6*d*. cloth extra, gilt edges.

Winged Life in the Tropics (from 'The Tropical World'). With 55 Illustrations. Crown 8vo. 2*s*. 6*d*. cloth extra, gilt edges.

Volcanoes and Earthquakes (from 'The Subterranean World'). With 30 Illustrations. Crown 8vo. 2*s*. 6*d*. cloth extra, gilt edges.

Wild Animals of the Tropics (from 'The Tropical World'). With 66 Illustrations. Crown 8vo. 3*s*. 6*d*. cloth extra, gilt edges.

By the Rev. J. G. Wood.

The Branch Builders (from 'Homes without Hands'). With 28 Illustrations. Crown 8vo. 2*s*. 6*d*. cloth extra, gilt edges.

Wild Animals of the Bible (from 'Bible Animals'). With 29 Illustrations. Crown 8vo. 3*s*. 6*d*. cloth extra, gilt edges.

Domestic Animals of the Bible (from 'Bible Animals'). With 23 Illustrations. Crown 8vo. 3*s*. 6*d*. cloth extra, gilt edges.

Bird Life of the Bible (from 'Bible Animals'). With 32 Illustrations. Crown 8vo. 3*s*. 6*d*. cloth extra, gilt edges.

Wonderful Nests (from 'Homes without Hands'). With 30 Illustrations. Crown 8vo. 3*s*. 6*d*. cloth extra, gilt edges.

Homes Under the Ground (from 'Homes without Hands'). With 28 Illustrations. Crown 8vo. 3*s*. 6*d*. cloth extra, gilt edges.

CHEMISTRY ENGINEERING, & GENERAL SCIENCE.

Arnott's Elements of Physics or Natural Philosophy. Crown 8vo. 12*s*. 6*d*.

Barrett's English Glees and Part-Songs : their Historical Development. Crown 8vo. 7*s*. 6*d*.

Bourne's Catechism of the Steam Engine. Crown 8vo. 7*s*. 6*d*.

— Handbook of the Steam Engine. Fcp. 8vo. 9*s*.

— Recent Improvements in the Steam Engine. Fcp. 8vo. 6*s*.

Buckton's Our Dwellings, Healthy and Unhealthy. Crown 8vo. 3*s*. 6*d*.

Clerk's The Gas Engine. With Illustrations. Crown 8vo. 7*s*. 6*d*.

Crookes's Select Methods in Chemical Analysis. 8vo. 24*s*.

Culley's Handbook of Practical Telegraphy. 8vo. 16*s*.

Fairbairn's Useful Information for Engineers. 3 vols. crown 8vo. 31*s*. 6*d*.

— Mills and Millwork. 1 vol. 8vo. 25*s*.

Ganot's Elementary Treatise on Physics, by Atkinson. Large crown 8vo. 15*s*.

— Natural Philosophy, by Atkinson. Crown 8vo. 7*s*. 6*d*.

Grove's Correlation of Physical Forces. 8vo. 15*s*.

Haughton's Six Lectures on Physical Geography. 8vo. 15*s*.

LONGMANS, GREEN, & CO., London and New York.

Helmholtz on the Sensations of Tone. Royal 8vo. 28s.

Helmholtz's Lectures on Scientific Subjects. 2 vols. crown 8vo. 7s. 6d. each.

Hudson and Gosse's The Rotifera or 'Wheel Animalcules.' With 30 Coloured Plates. 6 parts. 4to. 10s. 6d. each. Complete, 2 vols. 4to. £3. 10s.

Hullah's Lectures on the History of Modern Music. 8vo. 8s. 6d.

— Transition Period of Musical History. 8vo. 10s. 6d.

Jackson's Aid to Engineering Solution. Royal 8vo. 21s.

Jago's Inorganic Chemistry, Theoretical and Practical. Fcp. 8vo. 2s.

Jeans' Railway Problems. 8vo. 12s. 6d.

Kolbe's Short Text-Book of Inorganic Chemistry. Crown 8vo. 7s. 6d.

Lloyd's Treatise on Magnetism. 8vo. 10s. 6d.

Macalister's Zoology and Morphology of Vertebrate Animals. 8vo. 10s. 6d.

Macfarren's Lectures on Harmony. 8vo. 12s.

Miller's Elements of Chemistry, Theoretical and Practical. 3 vols. 8vo. Part I. Chemical Physics, 16s. Part II. Inorganic Chemistry, 24s. Part III. Organic Chemistry, price 31s. 6d.

Mitchell's Manual of Practical Assaying. 8vo. 31s. 6d.

Noble's Hours with a Three-inch Telescope. Crown 8vo. 4s. 6d.

Northcott's Lathes and Turning. 8vo. 18s.

Owen's Comparative Anatomy and Physiology of the Vertebrate Animals. 3 vols. 8vo. 73s. 6d.

Piesse's Art of Perfumery. Square crown 8vo. 21s.

Richardson's The Health of Nations; Works and Life of Edwin Chadwick, C.B. 2 vols. 8vo. 28s.

— The Commonhealth; a Series of Essays. Crown 8vo. 6s.

Schellen's Spectrum Analysis. 8vo. 31s. 6d.

Sennett's Treatise on the Marine Steam Engine. 8vo. 21s.

Smith's Air and Rain. 8vo. 24s.

Stoney's The Theory of the Stresses on Girders, &c. Royal 8vo. 36s.

Tilden's Practical Chemistry. Fcp. 8vo. 1s. 6d.

Tyndall's Faraday as a Discoverer. Crown 8vo. 3s. 6d.

— Floating Matter of the Air. Crown 8vo. 7s. 6d.

— Fragments of Science. 2 vols. post 8vo. 16s.

— Heat a Mode of Motion. Crown 8vo. 12s.

— Lectures on Light delivered in America. Crown 8vo. 5s.

— Lessons on Electricity. Crown 8vo. 2s. 6d.

— Notes on Electrical Phenomena. Crown 8vo. 1s. sewed, 1s. 6d. cloth.

— Notes of Lectures on Light. Crown 8vo. 1s. sewed, 1s. 6d. cloth.

— Sound, with Frontispiece and 203 Woodcuts. Crown 8vo. 10s. 6d.

Watts's Dictionary of Chemistry. 9 vols. medium 8vo. £15. 2s. 6d.

Wilson's Manual of Health-Science. Crown 8vo. 2s. 6d.

THEOLOGICAL AND RELIGIOUS WORKS.

Arnold's (Rev. Dr. Thomas) Sermons. 6 vols. crown 8vo. 5s. each.

Boultbee's Commentary on the 39 Articles. Crown 8vo. 6s.

Browne's (Bishop) Exposition of the 39 Articles. 8vo. 16s.

Bullinger's Critical Lexicon and Concordance to the English and Greek New Testament. Royal 8vo. 15s.

Colenso on the Pentateuch and Book of Joshua. Crown 8vo. 6s.

Conder's Handbook of the Bible. Post 8vo. 7s. 6d.

LONGMANS, GREEN, & CO., London and New York.

Conybeare & Howson's Life and Letters of St. Paul :—

Library Edition, with Maps, Plates, and Woodcuts. 2 vols. square crown 8vo. 21s.

Student's Edition, revised and condensed, with 46 Illustrations and Maps. 1 vol. crown 8vo. 7s. 6d.

Cox's (Homersham) The First Century of Christianity. 8vo. 12s.

Davidson's Introduction to the Study of the New Testament. 2 vols. 8vo. 30s.

Edersheim's Life and Times of Jesus the Messiah. 2 vols. 8vo. 24s.

— Prophecy and History in relation to the Messiah. 8vo. 12s.

Ellicott's (Bishop) Commentary on St. Paul's Epistles. 8vo. Corinthians I. 16s. Galatians, 8s. 6d. Ephesians, 8s. 6d. Pastoral Epistles, 10s. 6d. Philippians, Colossians and Philemon, 10s. 6d. Thessalonians, 7s. 6d.

— Lectures on the Life of our Lord. 8vo. 12s.

Ewald's Antiquities of Israel, translated by Solly. 8vo. 12s. 6d.

— History of Israel, translated by Carpenter & Smith. 8 vols. 8vo. Vols. 1 & 2, 24s. Vols. 3 & 4, 21s. Vol. 5, 18s. Vol. 6, 16s. Vol. 7, 21s. Vol. 8, 18s.

Hobart's Medical Language of St. Luke. 8vo. 16s.

Hopkins's Christ the Consoler. Fcp. 8vo. 2s. 6d.

Jukes's New Man and the Eternal Life. Crown 8vo. 6s.

— Second Death and the Restitution of all Things. Crown 8vo. 3s. 6d.

— Types of Genesis. Crown 8vo. 7s. 6d.

— The Mystery of the Kingdom. Crown 8vo. 3s. 6d.

Lenormant's New Translation of the Book of Genesis. Translated into English. 8vo. 10s. 6d.

Lyra Germanica : Hymns translated by Miss Winkworth. Fcp. 8vo. 5s.

Macdonald's (G.) Unspoken Sermons. Two Series. Crown 8vo. 3s. 6d. each.

— The Miracles of our Lord. Crown 8vo. 3s. 6d.

Manning's Temporal Mission of the Holy Ghost. Crown 8vo. 8s. 6d.

Martineau's Endeavours after the Christian Life. Crown 8vo. 7s. 6d.

— Hymns of Praise and Prayer. Crown 8vo. 4s. 6d. 32mo. 1s. 6d.

— Sermons, Hours of Thought on Sacred Things. 2 vols. 7s. 6d. each.

Monsell's Spiritual Songs for Sundays and Holidays. Fcp. 8vo. 5s. 18mo. 2s.

Müller's (Max) Origin and Growth of Religion. Crown 8vo. 7s. 6d.

— — Science of Religion. Crown 8vo. 7s. 6d.

Newman's Apologia pro Vitâ Suâ. Crown 8vo. 6s.

— The Idea of a University Defined and Illustrated. Crown 8vo. 7s.

— Historical Sketches. 3 vols. crown 8vo. 6s. each.

— Discussions and Arguments on Various Subjects. Crown 8vo. 6s.

— An Essay on the Development of Christian Doctrine. Crown 8vo. 6s.

— Certain Difficulties Felt by Anglicans in Catholic Teaching Considered. Vol. 1, crown 8vo. 7s. 6d. Vol. 2, crown 8vo. 5s. 6d.

— The Via Media of the Anglican Church, Illustrated in Lectures, &c. 2 vols. crown 8vo. 6s. each

— Essays, Critical and Historical. 2 vols. crown 8vo. 12s.

— Essays on Biblical and on Ecclesiastical Miracles. Crown 8vo. 6s.

— An Essay in Aid of a Grammar of Assent. 7s. 6d.

Overton's Life in the English Church (1660-1714). 8vo. 14s.

Supernatural Religion. Complete Edition. 3 vols. 8vo. 36s.

Younghusband's The Story of Our Lord told in Simple Language for Children. Illustrated. Crown 8vo. 2s. 6d. cloth plain ; 3s. 6d. cloth extra, gilt edges.

LONGMANS, GREEN, & CO., London and New York.

TRAVELS, ADVENTURES, &c.

Baker's Eight Years in Ceylon. Crown 8vo. 5s.

— Rifle and Hound in Ceylon. Crown 8vo. 5s.

Brassey's Sunshine and Storm in the East. Library Edition, 8vo. 21s. Cabinet Edition, crown 8vo. 7s. 6d. Popular Edition, 4to. 6d.

— Voyage in the 'Sunbeam.' Library Edition, 8vo. 21s. Cabinet Edition, crown 8vo. 7s. 6d. School Edition, fcp. 8vo. 2s. Popular Edition, 4to. 6d.

— In the Trades, the Tropics, and the 'Roaring Forties.' Library Edition, 8vo. 21s. Cabinet Edition, crown 8vo. 17s. 6d. Popular Edition, 4to. 6d.

Froude's Oceana ; or, England and her Colonies. Crown 8vo. 2s. boards ; 2s. 6d. cloth.

Howitt's Visits to Remarkable Places. Crown 8vo. 7s. 6d.

Riley's Athos ; or, The Mountain of the Monks. 8vo. 21s.

Three in Norway. By Two of Them. Illustrated. Crown 8vo. 2s. boards ; 2s. 6d. cloth.

WORKS OF FICTION.

Beaconsfield's (The Earl of) Novels and Tales. Hughenden Edition, with 2 Portraits on Steel and 11 Vignettes on Wood. 11 vols. crown 8vo. £2. 2s. Cheap Edition, 11 vols. crown 8vo. 1s. each, boards ; 1s. 6d. each, cloth.

Lothair.	Contarini Fleming.
Sybil.	Alroy, Ixion, &c.
Coningsby.	The Young Duke, &c.
Tancred.	Vivian Grey.
Venetia.	Endymion.
Henrietta Temple.	

Brabourne's (Lord) Friends and Foes from Fairyland. Crown 8vo. 6s.

Caddy's (Mrs.) Through the Fields with Linnæus : a Chapter in Swedish History. 2 vols. crown 8vo. 16s.

Gilkes' Boys and Masters. Crown 8vo. 3s. 6d.

Haggard's (H. Rider) She: a History of Adventure. Crown 8vo. 6s.

— Allan Quatermain. Illustrated. Crown 8vo. 6s.

Harte (Bret) On the Frontier. Three Stories. 16mo. 1s.

— — By Shore and Sedge. Three Stories. 16mo. 1s.

— — In the Carquinez Woods. Crown 8vo. 1s. boards ; 1s. 6d. cloth.

Lyall's (Edna) The Autobiography of a Slander. Fcp. 1s. sewed.

Melville's (Whyte) Novels. 8 vols. fcp. 8vo. 1s. each, boards ; 1s. 6d. each, cloth.

Digby Grand.	Good for Nothing.
General Bounce.	Holmby House.
Kate Coventry.	The Interpreter.
The Gladiators.	The Queen's Maries.

Molesworth's (Mrs.) Marrying and Giving in Marriage. Crown 8vo. 2s. 6d.

Novels by the Author of 'The Atelier du Lys':

The Atelier du Lys ; or, An Art Student in the Reign of Terror. Crown 8vo. 2s. 6d.

Mademoiselle Mori : a Tale of Modern Rome. Crown 8vo. 2s. 6d.

In the Olden Time: a Tale of the Peasant War in Germany. Crown 8vo. 2s. 6d.

Hester's Venture. Crown 8vo. 2s. 6d.

Oliphant's (Mrs.) Madam. Crown 8vo. 1s. boards ; 1s. 6d. cloth.

— — In Trust : the Story of a Lady and her Lover. Crown 8vo. 1s. boards ; 1s. 6d. cloth.

LONGMANS, GREEN, & CO., London and New York.

Payn's (James) The Luck of the Darrells. Crown 8vo. 1*s*. boards ; 1*s*. 6*d*. cloth.
— — Thicker than Water. Crown 8vo. 1*s*. boards ; 1*s*. 6*d*. cloth.
Reader's Fairy Prince Follow-my-Lead. Crown 8vo. 2*s*. 6*d*.
— The Ghost of Braukinshaw ; and other Tales. Fcp. 8vo. 2*s*. 6*d*.
Sewell's (Miss) Stories and Tales. Crown 8vo. 1*s*. each, boards ; 1*s*. 6*d*. cloth ;
  2*s*. 6*d*. cloth extra, gilt edges.

Amy Herbert. Cleve Hall.	A Glimpse of the World.
The Earl's Danghter.	Katharine Ashton.
Experience of Life.	Lanetou Parsonage.
Gertrude. Ivors.	Margaret Percival. Ursula.

Stevenson's (R. L.) The Dynamiter. Fcp. 8vo. 1*s*. sewed ; 1*s*. 6*d*. cloth.
— — Strange Case of Dr. Jekyll and Mr. Hyde. Fcp. 8vo. 1*s*.
  sewed ; 1*s*. 6*d*. cloth.
Sturgis' Thraldom : a Story. Crown 8vo. 6*s*.
Trollope's (Anthony) Novels. Fcp. 8vo. 1*s*. each, boards ; 1*s*. 6*d*. cloth.

The Warden	Barchester Towers.

POETRY AND THE DRAMA.

Armstrong's (Ed. J.) Poetical Works. Fcp. 8vo. 5*s*.
— (G. F.) Poetical Works :—

Poems, Lyrical and Dramatic. Fcp. 8vo. 6*s*.	King Saul. Fcp. 8vo. 5*s*.
	King David. Fcp. 8vo. 6*s*.
Ugone : a Tragedy. Fcp. 8vo. 6*s*.	King Solomon. Fcp. 8vo. 6*s*.
A Garland from Greece. Fcp. 8vo. 9*s*.	Stories of Wicklow. Fcp. 8vo. 9*s*.

Bowen's Harrow Songs and other Verses. Fcp. 8vo. 2*s*. 6*d*. ; or printed on
  hand-made paper, 5*s*.
Bowdler's Family Shakespeare. Medium 8vo. 14*s*. 6 vols. fcp. 8vo. 21*s*.
Dante's Divine Comedy, translated by James Innes Minchin. Crown 8vo. 15*s*.
Goethe's Faust, translated by Birds. Large crown 8vo. 12*s*. 6*d*.
— — translated by Webb. 8vo. 12*s*. 6*d*.
— — edited by Selss. Crown 8vo. 5*s*.
Ingelow's Poems. Vols. 1 and 2, fcp. 8vo. 12*s*.
— Lyrical and other Poems. Fcp. 8vo. 2*s*. 6*d*. cloth, plain ; 3*s*. cloth,
  gilt edges.
Macaulay's Lays of Ancient Rome, with Ivry and the Armada. Illustrated by
  Weguelin. Crown 8vo. 3*s*. 6*d*. gilt edges.
The same, Popular Edition. Illustrated by Scharf. Fcp. 4to. 6*d*. swd., 1*s*. cloth.
Nesbit's Lays and Legends. Crown 8vo. 5*s*.
Reader's Voices from Flowerland, a Birthday Book, 2*s*. 6*d*. cloth, 3*s*. 6*d*. roan.
Southey's Poetical Works. Medium 8vo. 14*s*.
Stevenson's A Child's Garden of Verses. Fcp. 8vo. 5*s*.
Virgil's Æneid, translated by Conington. Crown 8vo. 9*s*.
— Poems, translated into English Prose. Crown 8vo. 9*s*.

AGRICULTURE, HORSES, DOGS AND CATTLE.

Fitzwygram's Horses and Stables. 8vo. 5*s*.
Lloyd's The Science of Agriculture. 8vo. 12*s*.
Loudon's Encyclopædia of Agriculture. 21*s*.
Steel's Diseases of the Ox, a Manual of Bovine Pathology. 8vo. 15*s*.

LONGMANS, GREEN, & CO., London and New York.

Stonehenge's Dog in Health and Disease. Square crown 8vo. 7s. 6d,
—   Greyhound. Square crown 8vo. 15s.
Taylor's Agricultural Note Book. Fcp. 8vo. 2s. 6d.
Ville on Artificial Manures, by Crookes. 8vo. 21s.
Youatt's Work on the Dog. 8vo. 6s.
— — — — Horse. 8vo. 7s. 6d.

SPORTS AND PASTIMES.

The Badminton Library of Sports and Pastimes. Edited by the Duke of Beaufort
and A. E. T. Watson. With numerous Illustrations. Cr. 8vo. 10s. 6d. each.
Hunting, by the Duke of Beaufort, &c.
Fishing, by H. Cholmondeley-Pennell, &c. 2 vols.
Racing, by the Earl of Suffolk, &c.
Shooting, by Lord Walsingham, &c. 2 vols.
Cycling. By Visconut Bury.
⁎ *Other Volumes in preparation.*

Campbell-Walker's Correct Card, or How to Play at Whist. Fcp. 8vo. 2s. 6d.
Ford's Theory and Practice of Archery, revised by W. Butt. 8vo. 14s.
Francis's Treatise on Fishing in all its Branches. Post 8vo. 15s.
Longman's Chess Openings. Fcp. 8vo. 2s. 6d.
Pease's The Cleveland Hounds as a Trencher-Fed Pack. Royal 8vo. 18s.
Pole's Theory of the Modern Scientific Game of Whist. Fcp. 8vo. 2s. 6d.
Proctor's How to Play Whist. Crown 8vo. 5s.
Ronalds's Fly-Fisher's Entomology. 8vo. 14s.
Verney's Chess Eccentricities. Crown 8vo. 10s. 6d.
Wilcocks's Sea-Fisherman. Post 8vo. 6s.

ENCYCLOPÆDIAS, DICTIONARIES, AND BOOKS OF REFERENCE.

Acton's Modern Cookery for Private Families. Fcp. 8vo. 4s. 6d.
Ayre's Treasury of Bible Knowledge. Fcp. 8vo. 6s.
Brande's Dictionary of Science, Literature, and Art. 3 vols. medium 8vo. 63s.
Cabinet Lawyer (The), a Popular Digest of the Laws of England. Fcp. 8vo. 9s.
Cates's Dictionary of General Biography. Medium 8vo. 28s.
Gwilt's Encyclopædia of Architecture. 8vo. 52s. 6d.
Keith Johnston's Dictionary of Geography, or General Gazetteer. 8vo. 42s.
M'Culloch's Dictionary of Commerce and Commercial Navigation. 8vo. 63s.
Maunder's Biographical Treasury. Fcp. 8vo. 6s.
—   Historical Treasury. Fcp. 8vo. 6s.
—   Scientific and Literary Treasury. Fcp. 8vo. 6s.
—   Treasury of Bible Knowledge, edited by Ayre. Fcp. 8vo. 6s.
—   Treasury of Botany, edited by Lindley & Moore. Two Parts, 12s.
—   Treasury of Geography. Fcp. 8vo. 6s.
—   Treasury of Knowledge and Library of Reference. Fcp. 8vo. 6s.
—   Treasury of Natural History. Fcp 8vo. 6s.
Quain's Dictionary of Medicine. Medium 8vo. 31s. 6d., or in 2 vols. 34s.
Reeve's Cookery and Housekeeping. Crown 8vo. 7s. 6d.
Rich's Dictionary of Roman and Greek Antiquities. Crown 8vo. 7s. 6d.
Roget's Thesaurus of English Words and Phrases. Crown 8vo. 10s. 6d.
Willich's Popular Tables, by Marriott. Crown 8vo. 10s. 6d.

LONGMANS, GREEN, & CO., London and New York.

A SELECTION

OF

EDUCATIONAL WORKS.

TEXT-BOOKS OF SCIENCE

FULLY ILLUSTRATED.

Abney's Treatise on Photography. Fcp. 8vo. 3s. 6d.
Anderson's Strength of Materials. 3s. 6d.
Armstrong's Organic Chemistry. 3s. 6d.
Ball's Elements of Astronomy. 6s.
Barry's Railway Appliances. 3s. 6d.
Bauerman's Systematic Mineralogy. 6s.
— Descriptive Mineralogy. 6s.
Bloxam and Huntington's Metals. 5s.
Glazebrook's Physical Optics. 6s.
Glazebrook and Shaw's Practical Physics. 6s.
Gore's Art of Electro-Metallurgy. 6s.
Griffin's Algebra and Trigonometry. 3s. 6d.   Notes and Solutions, 3s. 6d.
Holmes's The Steam Engine. 6s.
Jenkin's Electricity and Magnetism. 3s. 6d.
Maxwell's Theory of Heat. 3s. 6d.
Merrifield's Technical Arithmetic and Mensuration. 3s. 6d. Key, 3s. 6d.
Miller's Inorganic Chemistry. 3s. 6d.
Preece and Sivewright's Telegraphy. 5s.
Rutley's Study of Rocks, a Text-Book of Petrology. 4s. 6d.
Shelley's Workshop Appliances. 4s. 6d.
Thomé's Structural and Physiological Botany. 6s.
Thorpe's Quantitative Chemical Analysis. 4s. 6d.
Thorpe and Muir's Qualitative Analysis. 3s. 6d.
Tilden's Chemical Philosophy. 3s. 6d. With Answers to Problems. 4s. 6d.
Unwin's Elements of Machine Design. 6s.
Watson's Plane and Solid Geometry. 3s. 6d.

THE GREEK LANGUAGE.

Bloomfield's College and School Greek Testament. Fcp. 8vo. 5s.
Bolland & Lang's Politics of Aristotle. Post 8vo. 7s. 6d.
Collis's Chief Tenses of the Greek Irregular Verbs. 8vo. 1s.
— Pontes Græci, Stepping-Stone to Greek Grammar. 12mo. 3s. 6d.
— Praxis Græca, Etymology. 12mo. 2s. 6d.
— Greek Verse-Book, Praxis Iambica. 12mo. 4s. 6d.
Farrar's Brief Greek Syntax and Accidence. 12mo. 4s. 6d.
— Greek Grammar Rules for Harrow School. 12mo. 1s. 6d.
Geare's Notes on Thucydides. Book I. Fcp. 8vo. 2s. 6d.
Hewitt's Greek Examination-Papers. 12mo. 1s. 6d.
Isbister's Xenophon's Anabasis, Books I. to III. with Notes. 12mo. 3s. 6d.
Jerram's Graece Reddenda. Crown 8vo. 1s. 6d.

LONGMANS, GREEN, & CO., London and New York.

Kennedy's Greek Grammar. 12mo. 4s. 6d.
Liddell & Scott's English-Greek Lexicon. 4to. 36s.; Square 12mo. 7s. 6d.
Mahaffy's Classical Greek Literature. Crown 8vo. Poets, 7s. 6d. Prose Writers,
    7s. 6d.
Morris's Greek Lessons. Square 18mo. Part I. 2s. 6d.; Part II. 1s.
Parry's Elementary Greek Grammar. 12mo. 3s. 6d.
Plato's Republic, Book I. Greek Text, English Notes by Hardy. Crown 8vo. 3s.
Sheppard and Evans's Notes on Thucydides. Crown 8vo. 7s. 6d.
Thucydides, Book IV. with Notes by Barton and Chavasse. Crown 8vo. 5s.
Valpy's Greek Delectus, improved by White. 12mo. 2s. 6d. Key, 2s. 6d.
White's Xenophon's Expedition of Cyrus, with English Notes. 12mo. 7s. 6d.
Wilkins's Manual of Greek Prose Composition. Crown 8vo. 5s. Key, 5s.
    —   Exercises in Greek Prose Composition. Crown 8vo. 4s. 6d. Key, 2s. 6d.
    —   New Greek Delectus. Crown 8vo. 3s. 6d. Key, 2s. 6d.
    —   Progressive Greek Delectus. 12mo. 4s. Key, 2s. 6d.
    —   Progressive Greek Anthology. 12mo. 5s.
    —   Scriptores Attici, Excerpts with English Notes. Crown 8vo. 7s. 6d.
    —   Speeches from Thucydides translated. Post 8vo. 6s.
Yonge's English-Greek Lexicon. 4to. 21s.; Square 12mo. 8s. 6d.

THE LATIN LANGUAGE.

Bradley's Latin Prose Exercises. 12mo. 3s. 6d. Key, 5s.
    —   Continuous Lessons in Latin Prose. 12mo. 5s. Key, 5s. 6d.
    —   Cornelius Nepos, improved by White. 12mo. 3s. 6d.
    —   Eutropius, improved by White. 12mo. 2s. 6d.
    —   Ovid's Metamorphoses, improved by White. 12mo. 4s. 6d.
    —   Select Fables of Phædrus, improved by White. 12mo. 2s. 6d.
Collis's Chief Tenses of Latin Irregular Verbs. 8vo. 1s.
    —   Pontes Latini, Stepping-Stone to Latin Grammar. 12mo. 3s. 6d.
Hewitt's Latin Examination-Papers. 12mo. 1s. 6d.
Isbister's Cæsar, Books I.-VII. 12mo. 4s.; or with Reading Lessons, 4s. 6d.
    —   Cæsar's Commentaries, Books I.-V. 12mo. 3s. 6d.
    —   First Book of Cæsar's Gallic War. 12mo. 1s. 6d.
Jerram's Latiné Reddenda. Crown 8vo. 1s. 6d.
Kennedy's Child's Latin Primer, or First Latin Lessons. 12mo. 2s.
    —   Child's Latin Accidence. 12mo. 1s.
    —   Elementary Latin Grammar. 12mo. 3s. 6d.
    —   Elementary Latin Reading Book, or Tirocinium Latinum. 12mo. 2s.
    —   Latin Prose, Palæstra Stili Latiui. 12mo. 6s.
    —   Latin Vocabulary. 12mo. 2s. 6d.
    —   Subsidia Primaria, Exercise Books to the Public School Latin Primer.
            I. Accidence and Simple Construction, 2s. 6d. II. Syntax, 3s. 6d.
    —   Key to the Exercises in Subsidia Primaria, Parts I. and II. price 5s.
    —   Subsidia Primaria, III. the Latin Compound Sentence. 12mo. 1s.
    —   Curriculum Stili Latini. 12mo. 4s. 6d. Key, 7s. 6d.
    —   Palæstra Latina, or Second Latin Reading Book. 12mo. 5s.

LONGMANS, GREEN, & CO., London and New York.

Millington's Latin Prose Composition. Crown 8vo. 3s. 6d.
— Selections from Latin Prose. Crown 8vo. 2s. 6d.
Moody's Eton Latin Grammar. 12mo. 2s. 6d. The Accidence separately, 1s.
Morris's Elementa Latina. Fcp. 8vo. 1s. 6d. Key, 2s. 6d.
Parry's Origines Romanæ, from Livy, with English Notes. Crown 8vo. 4s.
The Public School Latin Primer. 12mo. 2s. 6d.
— — — — Grammar, by Rev. Dr. Kennedy. Post 8vo. 7s. 6d.
Prendergast's Mastery Series, Manual of Latin. 12mo. 2s. 6d.
Rapier's Introduction to Composition of Latin Verse. 12mo. 3s. 6d. Key, 2s. 6d.
Sheppard and Turner's Aids to Classical Study. 12mo. 5s. Key, 6s.
Valpy's Latin Delectus, improved by White. 12mo. 2s. 6d. Key, 3s. 6d.
Virgil's Æneid, translated into English Verse by Conington. Crown 8vo. 9s.
— Works, edited by Kennedy. Crown 8vo. 10s. 6d.
— — translated into English Prose by Conington. Crown 8vo. 9s.
Walford's Progressive Exercises in Latin Elegiac Verse. 12mo. 2s. 6d. Key, 5s.
White and Riddle's Large Latin-English Dictionary. 1 vol. 4to. 21s.
White's Concise Latin-Eng. Dictionary for University Students. Royal 8vo. 12s.
— Junior Students' Eng.-Lat. & Lat.-Eng. Dictionary. Square 12mo. 5s.

Separately { The Latin-English Dictionary, price 3s.
{ The English-Latin Dictionary, price 3s.

Yonge's Latin Gradus. Post 8vo. 9s.; or with Appendix, 12s.

WHITE'S GRAMMAR-SCHOOL GREEK TEXTS.

Æsop (Fables) & Palæphatus (Myths). 32mo. 1s.
Euripides, Hecuba. 2s.
Homer, Iliad, Book I. 1s.
— Odyssey, Book I. 1s.
Lucian, Select Dialogues. 1s.
Xenophon, Anabasis, Books I. III. IV. V. & VI. 1s. 6d. each ; Book II. 1s.; Book VII. 2s.

Xenophon, Book I. without Vocabulary. 3d.
St. Matthew's and St. Luke's Gospels. 2s. 6d. each.
St. Mark's and St. John's Gospels. 1s. 6d. each.
The Acts of the Apostles. 2s. 6d.
St. Paul's Epistle to the Romans. 1s. 6d.

The Four Gospels in Greek, with Greek-English Lexicon. Edited by John T. White, D.D. Oxon. Square 32mo. price 5s.

WHITE'S GRAMMAR-SCHOOL LATIN TEXTS.

Cæsar, Gallic War, Books I. & II. V. & VI. 1s. each. Book I. without Vocabulary, 3d.
Cæsar, Gallic War, Books III. & IV. 9d. each.
Cæsar, Gallic War, Book VII. 1s. 6d.
Cicero, Cato Major (Old Age). 1s. 6d.
Cicero, Lælius (Friendship). 1s. 6d.
Eutropius, Roman History, Books I. & II. 1s. Books III. & IV. 1s.
Horace, Odes, Books I. II. & IV. 1s. each.
Horace, Odes, Book III. 1s. 6d.
Horace, Epodes and Carmen Seculare. 1s.

Nepos, Miltiades, Simon, Pausanias, Aristides. 9d.
Ovid. Selections from Epistles and Fasti. 1s.
Ovid, Select Myths from Metamorphoses. 9d.
Phædrus, Select Easy Fables,
Phædrus, Fables, Books I. & II. 1s.
Sallust, Bellum Catilinarium. 1s. 6d.
Virgil, Georgics, Book IV. 1s.
Virgil, Æneid, Books I. to VI. 1s. each. Book I. without Vocabulary. 3d.
Virgil, Æneid, Books VII. VIII. X. XI. XII. 1s. 6d. each.

LONGMANS, GREEN, & CO., London and New York.

THE FRENCH LANGUAGE.

Albités's How to Speak French. Fcp. 8vo. 5s. 6d.
— Instantaneous French Exercises. Fcp. 2s. Key, 2s.
Cassal's French Genders. Crown 8vo. 3s. 6d.
Cassal & Karcher's Graduated French Translation Book. Part I. 3s. 6d.
    Part II. 5s. Key to Part I. by Professor Cassal, price 5s.
Contanseau's Practical French and English Dictionary. Post 8vo. 3s. 6d.
— Pocket French and English Dictionary. Square 18mo. 1s. 6d.
— Premières Lectures. 12mo. 2s. 6d.
— First Step in French. 12mo. 2s. 6d. Key, 3s.
— French Accidence. 12mo. 2s. 6d.
— — Grammar. 12mo. 4s. Key, 3s.
Contanseau's Middle-Class French Course. Fcp. 8vo. :—

Accidence, 8d.	French Translation-Book, 8d.
Syntax, 8d.	Easy French Delectus, 8d.
French Conversation-Book, 8d.	First French Reader, 8d.
First French Exercise-Book, 8d.	Second French Reader, 8d.
Second French Exercise-Book, 8d.	French and English Dialogues, 8d.

Contanseau's Guide to French Translation. 12mo. 3s. 6d. Key 3s. 6d.
— Prosateurs et Poètes Français. 12mo. 5s.
— Précis de la Littérature Française. 12mo. 3s. 6d.
— Abrégé de l'Histoire de France. 12mo. 2s. 6d.
Féval's Chouans et Bleus, with Notes by C. Sankey, M.A. Fcp. 8vo. 2s. 6d.
Jerram's Sentences for Translation into French. Cr. 8vo. 1s. Key, 2s. 6d.
Prendergast's Mastery Series, French. 12mo. 2s. 6d.
Souvestre's Philosophe sous les Toits, by Stiévenard. Square 18mo. 1s. 6d.
Stepping-Stone to French Pronunciation. 18mo. 1s.
Stiévenard's Lectures Françaises from Modern Authors. 12mo. 4s. 6d.
— Rules and Exercises on the French Language. 12mo. 3s. 6d.
Tarver's Eton French Grammar. 12mo. 6s. 6d.

THE GERMAN LANGUAGE.

Blackley's Practical German and English Dictionary. Post 8vo. 3s. 6d.
Buchheim's German Poetry, for Repetition. 18mo. 1s. 6d.
Collis's Card of German Irregular Verbs. 8vo. 2s.
Fischer-Fischart's Elementary German Grammar. Fcp. 8vo. 2s. 6d.
Just's German Grammar. 12mo. 1s. 6d.
— German Reading Book. 12mo. 3s. 6d.
Longman's Pocket German and English Dictionary. Square 18mo. 2s. 6d.
Naftel's Elementary German Course for Public Schools. Fcp. 8vo.

German Accidence. 9d.	German Prose Composition Book. 9d.
German Syntax. 9d.	First German Reader. 9d.
First German Exercise-Book. 9d.	Second German Reader. 9d.
Second German Exercise-Book. 9d.	

Prendergast's Mastery Series, German. 12mo. 2s. 6d.
Quick's Essentials of German. Crown 8vo. 3s. 6d.
Selss's School Edition of Goethe's Faust. Crown 8vo. 5s.
— Outline of German Literature. Crown 8vo. 4s. 6d.
Wirth's German Chit-Chat. Crown 8vo. 2s. 6d.

LONGMANS, GREEN, & CO., London and New York.

Spottiswoode & Co. Printers, New-street Square, London.

www.ingramcontent.com/pod-product-compliance
Lightning Source LLC
Chambersburg PA
CBHW031037120726
47905CB00007B/2221